For Sophie, my Fury.

Model Railway Apocalypse

Copyright © 2024 Luke James

All rights reserved

No part of this book may be reproduced, or stored in a retrieval system, or transmitted in any form or by any means, electronic, mechanical, photocopying, recording, or otherwise, without express written permission of the author.

Model Railway
Apocalypse

**An Off-The-Rails Apocalyptic
Love Story**

Luke James

CONTENTS

09 | Prologue

11 | Chapter One

19 | Chapter Two

25 | Chapter Three

33 | Chapter Four

41 | Chapter Five

47 | Chapter Six

57 | Chapter Seven

63 | Chapter Eight

69 | Chapter Nine

73 | Chapter Ten

77 | Chapter Eleven

83 | Chapter Twelve

89 | Chapter Thirteen

93 | Chapter Fourteen

97 | Chapter Fifteen

101 | Chapter Sixteen

109 | Chapter Seventeen

117 | Chapter Eighteen

123 | Chapter Nineteen

131 | Chapter Twenty

139 | Chapter Twenty-One

145 | Chapter Twenty-Two

151 | Chapter Twenty-Three

161 | Chapter Twenty-Four

163 | Chapter Twenty-Five

167 | Chapter Twenty-Six

171 | Chapter Twenty-Seven

179 | Chapter Twenty-Eight

183 | Epilogue

189 | Acknowledgements

191 | About the Author

Do not go gentle into that good night.
Rage, rage against the dying of the light.

\- Dylan Thomas

Luke James

PROLOGUE

He could hear the big black steam locomotive still laughing at him. Alone, perched on the fallen body of the giant robot, face smeared with coal and flannel robe stained with a cocktail of shark and dinosaur guts, Norman surveyed the toy box of nightmares around him. An unnatural green glow spilled out of the river and mangled corpses were sprawled across the banks, mutated and contorted. The hills, once the colour of spring, were coated with ash, and lava still oozed sluggishly from the highest peak.

How long had he been here now? Counting days was difficult when there had only been darkness for so long. When had he last seen daylight?

He couldn't see anyone left alive, but disembodied groans told him they were out there, in the shadows beyond the whispering train wreck – lost souls with no say over their fate. In a way they were his children, and he was their God, stripped of power and banished to live among his creations.

How long had it been?

Too long. He'd run out of hope.

He slid off the deceased mechanoid and began his walk to the edge of the world.

Luke James

CHAPTER ONE

Fury poured hot tea into two flowery patterned china teacups and watched the rising steam with fascination. It always reminded her of the old days, back in Hell, when she used to scorch damned souls. But today she was in the kitchen, waiting for the timer to ping on a Victoria sponge. Staring into the oven, she was determined it would come out right this time.

She smelled smoke. Not the something-burning kind, but the cloud-of-cigarette-fumes kind.

"Oh, it breaks my heart to see my daughter being so domesticated," Ferocity announced, stepping out of her dimensional gate. "What immortal in their right mind would watch an oven timer so closely?"

Fury was used to her mother's snide remarks. She heard them most days. Turning her back on her family dynasty in one of the outlying regions of Hell, Fury had embraced life on Earth and her marriage to the human Norman. Her family and friends had all warned her about trying to live among humans; many demons had tried, and each one - sooner or later - had changed their minds and caught the fast train back to fiery paradise. But Fury was proving to be an exception. She'd been married to Norman for twenty two years, which was nothing compared to an eternity in Hell, but in human terms, it was a long time and she was proud of that. It certainly hadn't been easy with her demon mother constantly trying to convince her to "ditch the wretch and come home."

Model Railway Apocalypse

"Morning, mother." Fury sighed. "No one is telling you to look." She used the same response every time Ferocity voiced the same old disapprovals. "Yet here you still are."

"You bet I am. Where is the miserable mortal?" Ferocity tended to appear when Norman wasn't around.

"He's in the spare room working on his train-set."

Ferocity cackled.

"Pathetic."

"I think it's sweet, Mother. I like that he's passionate about something."

"And where's your passion? I've seen you torturing the dead with a grin the size of a freight train. I've seen you brand men with red-hot pokers and snap them with stretching racks while laughing your horns off. Girl, you were an artist! And now look at you, old and subservient, making tea for a mortal weakling who still plays with toys. He's the toy! It's simple nature. This marriage is unnatural."

Fury did her best to ignore Ferocity. She watched the oven anxiously, waiting for the kitchen timer to ring. When she came to Earth, she had taken human form - easily done with a flick of magic. It was a common trick employed during the torture process – taking on the appearance of someone they hated, or worse, someone they loved.

Often, when it was just her and Norman, Fury would slide into her demon form. It was more comfortable, like putting on an old cardigan - although that analogy distorted how terrifying her appearance would be to the average human. Not to Norman, though. He didn't bat an eyelid when she slipped into her old skin. In fact, he never failed to tell her how beautiful she was, whatever her exterior.

Luke James

"If I may say so, you're looking especially old and decrepit these days," Ferocity taunted.

Fury deliberately aged her appearance. Being immortal, she'd stopped aging when she reached adulthood eight-hundred years ago. But a flick of magic made her look only a few years younger than Norman, who was now sixty-one.

"You know King Rage's second-born son has extended an invitation to take you as his Hellbride? You could go back to being young and beautiful... like me."

"You'd have a comfortable and fulfilling life married to Prince Plague. You wouldn't want for anything."

"I don't want for anything now. I'm perfectly happy."

"But what will you do when your pitiful husband dies of old age?"

Fury knew Ferocity hoped she would return to her younger-looking demon-self and they could be more like sisters, like most demon mother-daughters. She was getting impatient, made worse by Fury's foolish defiance.

"I hope your nauseating contempt for your heritage isn't rubbing off on my granddaughter. Yes, I'm sure our family's judiciousness simply skipped a generation."

"Malice is growing up to be a much wiser individual than either of us, Mother. I'm sure she's perfectly capable of choosing her own path."

Malice was Fury and Norman's twenty one year-old daughter. They called her Malice because it was demon tradition to name offspring after what humans would call "negative" nouns. Norman hadn't been keen on honouring that tradition, but Fury had turned her back on her demon life to marry him, so Malice was a compromise – after all, Malice was similar to Alice, which had been his mother's name.

Model Railway Apocalypse

Demon genes were dominant. Malice had all the advantages of her mother's kind, including immortality. Fury taught her to change her appearance when she was very young, which had been traumatic for the girl, and then there were the tempestuous teenage years when she raised hell wrestling with her inner demoness. But she'd weathered those trials to become a well-adjusted individual.

"Fine! I see you're in one of your ridiculous stubborn moods. But know this: Plague won't wait around forever."

The kitchen timer rang and Fury opened the oven. She coughed as smoke poured out – her tolerance for it, a natural symptom of growing up in Hell, had faded since she'd been on Earth. She removed the cake; it was burnt black.

Ferocity cackled.

"You see, my dear, you were raised to scorch and burn! It's who you are!"

"Goodbye, Mother," Fury said, gazing glumly down at her destroyed creation.

Ferocity was still chortling as she vanished, leaving her usual toxic aroma behind.

Norman was putting the finishing touches to the vast and elegant miniature world. Wearing dusty clothes reserved for painting and sculpting, and magnifying lenses strapped over his eyes, making them look the size of tennis balls, he used a set of tweezers to manoeuvre the last people - a barmaid and a merry patron holding a pint of stout - into place inside an English country pub.

One after the other, Norman had lost both of his parents as a young adult; since then he'd developed what you might call an "addictive personality". At one stage

Luke James

or another, he'd become obsessed with everything from birdwatching to kite-surfing, photography to gardening, Japanese film to Italian cooking. His entire adult life, he'd used every hour of his free time to learn, practise, build, create, explore and observe. He was used to the eye-rolling from his wife and daughter, every time he discovered a new passion. Of course they meant it affectionately. Besides, there were worse addictions than those in his ever-expanding gallery.

So when his company was making cut-backs, forcing him into early retirement, Norman was elated. The HR manager was baffled by his euphoric reaction, watching him victory-dance out the door.

On his last day, as soon as he got home, he began drawing up plans for a model railway. Six months later, he finally stood back and observed his creation, which lay waiting for the final spark of life. Two steam engines sat on the tracks, ready to spring into action at the push of a button and tour around the rural-themed town; in and out of the station and depot, through tunnels and green hills, over bridges and the glistening river. Buses and cars lined the roads. Dozens of buildings were meticulously positioned and embedded in the hand-sculpted natural landscape, mimicking the authentic development and expansion of a rural town. Norman didn't care much for historical accuracy, working only under the remit that it should be a place he'd want to live. The scene was peppered with flourishes of springtime: patches of bluebells and daffodils; blossom in the trees; lambs and calves among the livestock in the emerald meadows; a fairground in a park surrounded by shops and houses and cottages. There was even a duck pond. Norman had paid so much attention to the details that miniature people could be

Model Railway Apocalypse

seen in the windows of some buildings.

The model itself was suspended about a meter off the floor and took up most of the generously sized bedroom, with just a narrow gap around the perimeter so he could reach everywhere on the model. In the corner of the room was a workstation with his various tools and materials for painting and sculpting.

"You okay, dear?" Fury asked, walking up behind him with a tray of tea and biscuits. She couldn't help but smile as Norman jumped at her voice, engrossed in what he was doing.

"Wonderful," he said, looking at her through kind eyes, magnified behind the thick lenses. He lifted them off his head. Fury was always startled by the way human eyes aged. The evidence of Norman's mortality was getting harder to ignore each day: the narrow squint, the deep, spreading smile lines, like crags in the desert. She struggled to keep up with his fall from youth. It often filled her with dread. At least if he was a rampant sinner - a serial killer or molester - she'd be able return to Hell to be with him. Maybe even try to protect him. But Norman was almost guaranteed to go the other way.

With his arm around her, he invited her to admire his creation.

"It looks incredible, Norm. Is it finished?"

"I think so." He pushed a button on the control box and the trains sprang to life. He pushed another button and the fairground became animated; the Ferris wheel turned, the carousel spun and the swing boats swayed to and fro.

Fury put her palm to her chest. "It's lovely."

"That's not all," Norman said. "Switch off the lights." She obliged, blanketing the room in darkness.

Luke James

He flicked another switch on the control box; all the buildings and fairground lit up. Fury gasped at the glowing scene. She held her hand over her mouth. The enthusiasm and the attention to detail reflected exactly what she loved about her husband.

"I used LED lights," Norman said.

"It's magical," Fury said. "I'm so impressed."

"It's called Furydale." Norman turned the lights back on and pointed at one of the road signs.

Fury hugged him, wondering how she could thank him.

"When I was a boy my dad had a trainset," Norman said. "Sometimes, when he let me play with it, I used to pretend the people were alive. I'd imagine I was one of them and I could walk around exploring the miniature world. My dad got rid of it when we moved house. I begged him not to, but he said we didn't have the space. I swore to myself that one day I'd build my own, and it would be the most beautiful model railway in the world."

"And now you've done it," Fury said.

"Well, I'm sure there are better ones. But it's good enough for me."

That's it. Fury clicked her fingers as the most perfect idea came to her. She knew exactly how to repay the generous tribute that Norman had just given her.

In Hell she'd mastered the powers to cause suffering. They were limited only by her imagination. But pleasure and pain shared the same nerves; experience of one was intensified by acknowledgement of the other. As such, Fury also had the powers to bring pleasure, in whatever form she could imagine it.

She rolled up her skirt.

"What are you doing, my love?" Norman asked.

She uncoiled her demon tail which, being the source

of her magic, she kept even in her human form, hidden beneath her skirts and dresses. She swung it back and forth, before whipping it towards Norman's wrist.

"Put that away, Angel," Norman said, playfully. He always called her Angel, even though she was a demon. And he always knew she was up to something when she got her tail out.

It wrapped around his wrist several times.

She winked at him and then nodded with one deliberate movement. The loving couple vanished.

CHAPTER TWO

Norman rubbed his eyes in disbelief. It hadn't taken him long to recognise where he was. The sign above one shop read: "Furydale General Store". He couldn't believe how the town had come to life: the people were moving and interacting; the sky was blue; the steam trains produced real steam; even the cars were moving, driven by real people.

"This is how God must feel," Norman said, eyes wide and child-like, taking in the sight of a huge locomotive as it peeped and whistled over the level-crossing at the centre of town. He recognised it as a life-sized version of his model train, The Phoenix. The smell of burning coal was so powerful he could taste it.

Fury chuckled at the sight of her enamoured husband. He turned to face her and his eyes widened even further – she was young again, the age she'd been when they met.

"You're beautiful," he said, taking her by the hands.

"You look pretty good yourself," Fury said, raising his hands up to his eye level, forcing him to look at his own hands. They were smooth, and glowing with youth. He rubbed the tips of his fingers together. They were soft. He brought his warm palms up to his cheek. Even his face was smooth.

They were standing in the park. On one side the fairground was teeming. On the other families sat by the pond eating picnics while children threw a stick for a collie. Over the hedgerow the street was bustling.

Model Railway Apocalypse

Norman walked in circles, mouth wide open. Fury followed closely, amused by her husband. All the items he'd taken such care over had come to life, including the ducks quacking in the pond and the fishermen perched by the river.

"What do you think?" Fury asked.

"It's wonderful. I mean, I've seen you use your magic before, but this is something else.... How the...." His voice trailed off as he took in more of the details: the farm up on the hillside; fields populated by sheep; the authenticity of the people going about their lives.

"I'm glad you like it. Let's go for a drink," she said, pointing to the pub. Norman had named the miniature building "The Shaggy Dog" in remembrance of his childhood pet. "Puddles" didn't seem like a good name for a pub.

Although Norman's sculpting of the building interiors in his model had been limited, the details had been fleshed out by Fury's magic, and it was exactly how he'd imagined it. Inside The Shaggy Dog the ceilings were low and the bar was well stocked, furnished with a mix of large oak tables, dining chairs and arm chairs. There was black and white framed photography on the walls and a log fire burned in the corner, adding to the cosy atmosphere. Even the barmaid was exactly like the model woman he'd just positioned: a pale redhead in her early forties, face caked in make-up, huge breasts barely hidden by a partially unbuttoned white blouse with a gutsy red bra underneath. He'd kept that creative indulgence to himself, and wondered how Fury had been able to extract all these details from his imagination. He took Fury's hand and led her to the bar.

"What can I get for you, lovelies?" the barmaid asked.

Luke James

"A glass of house red," Fury said.

"And for you, handsome?"

Norman felt a little anxious at the barmaid's flirtations, but he put on his best gentleman's manner: "A Stormy Sea, please."

"What's that, sweetheart?"

Nervously, Norman turned to Fury, who had let her smile slip. She stared at the barmaid coldly.

"A shot of dark rum over ginger beer and ice," he said.

"One shot?"

"Make it two," Norman said.

The barmaid fetched the drinks and declared they were "on the house for the handsome gentleman and his beautiful wife," which was lucky because Norman realised he didn't have his wallet with him. He thanked her politely and the couple headed over to two vacant armchairs located next to the crackling fire. As they sat down Fury commented on how "friendly" the barmaid had been.

"If I didn't know better I might've thought they named the pub after her," Fury said.

"How have you done all this?" Norman asked his wife.

"Yours is not to know how," Fury replied with a satisfied smile. "Yours is to enjoy."

Norman grinned.

"I mean, this is almost exactly how I imagined it when I built it." He was careful to add the "almost" given the behaviour and appearance of the barmaid. "How did you know?"

"When you pour so much creative energy into something, it's like breathing life into it. It takes on a mind of its own. You've heard writers describe the feeling of characters coming to life in their imagination, and stories writing themselves. It's the same thing here. You've nurtured your

Model Railway Apocalypse

imaginative world with such devotion; the essence of that creative energy has grown into a living and breathing entity, filling in the rest of the details for you. I may have ignited the fuse, but you created the essence with which it burns."

"Thank you, my love. This is a dream come true."

Norman spotted a sign above the bar which read: "Rooms available."

"I have a perfect idea!" he said.

"What's that?"

"Let's take a holiday! Here! Tonight! We can check in to the Bed & Breakfast and spend a few days here in Furydale. No long journeys. No aeroplanes. We could just come here. What do you reckon?" Norman struggled to contain his excitement.

"That sounds like a wonderful idea."

"Great! Let's go and pack our bags!" he said, getting out of his chair.

"But there's a problem, Norm."

Norman's face dropped. He should have known there'd be a catch. He didn't fully understand Fury's powers, and half expected her to tell him the magic she'd used for this latest miracle was so advanced that it would soon run out and they would only be able stay until midnight, or some fairy-tale caveat like that. He sat back down, bracing himself for disappointment.

"You're forgetting Malice is going to phone this evening. She's been away with Henry, remember? Before they went she was convinced he was going to propose. You don't want to miss her big news, do you?"

"You never know, he might not have popped the question."

"I'm not willing to take that chance. I want to be there

Luke James

for her if she does have exciting news, don't you?"

Norman couldn't argue without seeming like a terrible father. He nodded.

"It's a wonderful idea," Fury said, sensing his frustration. "We can still do it. Let's just do it tomorrow instead. That'll give us more time to pack. And we can tell Malice that we're going away for a few days."

Norman's face glowed again. "Yeah, and I can make some final improvements to the town! I've had a couple of ideas of things I can add, just finishing touches to make the place perfect."

Later in the evening, when Malice phoned, Norman was so absorbed by the potential of exploring his miniature world that he barely registered his daughter's announcement; as predicted, she was engaged to her long term boyfriend, Henry. On any other day Norman would have been overjoyed, but today his fatherly pride paled next to his utter exhilaration at returning to Furydale. He was even slightly annoyed about the bride-to-be and her fiancé inviting themselves to stay in a couple of days' time, limiting his and Fury's stay in Furydale. They lived a two and a half hour drive away, so visits happened only every few weeks.

"Couldn't they come a couple of days later?" Norman asked.

"They're eager to celebrate with us. We can't deny them," Fury said.

As soon as they'd returned from the miniature world he'd set about making modifications. He added a café next to the general store, a little bookshop next to the café, a butcher and an indoor swimming pool. He also made an adjustment to the town hall so it doubled up as

Model Railway Apocalypse

an independent cinema for watching old films. He hoped he and Fury would have everything they needed to enjoy a few days in the idyllic community. He had also added a florist next to the bakery so he could buy flowers and croissants for his wife.

Norman worked into the night adding features to the model world. When he went to bed, he fell asleep with a smile.

Luke James

CHAPTER THREE

"How domesticated and booorrrring," Ferocity said, stepping out of her usual cloud of smoke into the master bedroom where Fury was packing. Norman had wanted to check the adjustments he'd made to the town so he'd convinced Fury to send him back into the miniature world, before she joined him later in the afternoon. He wanted everything to be perfect for their holiday.

"Morning, Mother," Fury replied in her usual pleasant tone, searching the drawer for her bikini.

"You're leaving him?' Ferocity said, spotting the suitcase. 'Thank Lucifer! Let me help you pack." She picked up the bedside lamp and tried fitting it into the suitcase without even unplugging it.

"No!" Fury said, snatching the lamp back. "We're going away for a couple of days."

"Damn!"

"And your granddaughter is getting married."

"No!" she gasped, shaking her head. "Wrong. Wrong. Wrong! I don't know what to be more appalled by. Who's she marrying? Not that mortal worm who's been hanging around her for years?"

Fury smiled.

"Curse her bones! Does he even know the truth about her?"

"Yes. And he respects it. You won't have any secrets to threaten her with."

"Everything about your life disgusts me," Ferocity said.

Model Railway Apocalypse

"I'm sorry to cause you so much offence, Mother, but I accepted your disapproval of my life choices a long time ago."

"I just wish your daughter didn't share your contemptuousness!"

Fury felt a surge of anger. "If you want to hang around here and insult me, fine, but don't you dare insult my daughter, or I'll cast you back into Hell!"

"I knew my daughter was in there," Ferocity said with a smile. "There's the passion you've missed."

Fury turned to the large mirror on her wardrobe door and observed her inadvertent transformation. Her eyes flared with a fiery red and her skin shimmered with an icy blue hue. She shook it off and returned to her aged human form, embarrassed that she'd given her mother ammunition.

"You can't cast me out, remember. Your magic won't work on me – I know your secret, my girl."

Demons could use their magic on other demons, but knowing a demon's secret meant immunity from their powers.

"So you're always reminding me. But still you keep it, afraid I'll exile you from my home the moment you're no longer protected."

"Maybe someday I'll take the chance. When the truth is out, this may not be your home at all. It's quite poetic really – the thing that brought you and your mortal toy together could well be the thing that tears you apart."

"Get out!"

Ferocity was satisfied.

"Fine. I hope you have a truly delightful holiday with your sad, old husband."

She vanished.

Luke James

Fury entered the spare room carrying her suitcase, ready to join Norman in Furydale. Like Norman, she had been excited about the holiday. Maybe not on the same level as her husband, but seeing him so happy made her happy. Plus, she always enjoyed a change of scenery. But she felt rattled after her confrontation with Ferocity. She'd grown used to interference from her mother, who she did truly love, but her anger at the criticism of her daughter had taken her by surprise. She felt real fury for the first time in years, and it stirred in her now, as if waking from a long slumber, not ready to go dormant just yet.

She was also agitated by her mother's suggestion that her life had become passionless. No matter how much she denied it, deep down she knew she'd lost something. Passion came in many forms. Fury felt passionately about her husband and daughter, about their happiness and welfare. She could see passion in them, and feel she somehow shared in it. But she no longer felt the same kind of thrill she experienced when she was torturing people in Hell. It was what she was raised to do, and she'd learnt to love it more than most. She'd turned her back on that when she left, lured by her emergent affection for Norman.

Then there was lust. Fury had accepted that Norman's libido had faded in recent years, but an immortal's carnal desire was rarely quelled, and hers was simmering beneath the surface.

She took a deep breath and shrugged off her ruminations. Maybe this holiday will help, she told herself, as she zapped into the miniature town.

Appearing in the middle of the park, which was once again buzzing with life, Fury glanced around at the buildings. There was the B & B where she was to meet Norman. There was the bakery and general store. She

Model Railway Apocalypse

couldn't help but smile when she noticed the addition of the florist and the bookshop. She spotted a poster for the town hall-cum-cinema on a nearby lamp post. It read: "Playing tonight: Frank Capra's It Happened One Night starring Clark Gable & Claudette Colbert." That was her favourite film. She couldn't wait to see it again. Finally she saw a sign for the swimming pool, pointing down the road away from the park. She cursed. After being rattled by her mother, she'd forgotten her swimming things. Better to go back and get them now than interrupt their minibreak.

Ferocity was also riled. It wasn't like Fury to lose her temper; she would know - having tried to grill it out of her nearly every day since her dear daughter decided to live sheep-like among humans. As saddened as she was by seeing her upset, she was more disturbed by the news that even her granddaughter was going to marry a mortal man. Upsetting Fury was unfortunate but it acted as a spur to Ferocity to landing some damaging blows to her chosen way of life, which was why she now morphed herself into a spider and perched on the walls. She observed her daughter as she materialised out of the model railway.

Strange that she should appear young again, she thought, as she watched Fury leave the spare room. Maybe she could use that somehow.

Having checked into the Bed & Breakfast above The Shaggy Dog, Norman entered Room 7 and, even before setting down his suitcase and the bouquet of flowers he'd just bought for Fury, began admiring the furnishings. The Queen-sized bed was covered in cream Egyptian cotton sheets, paired with light and airy curtains which floated in the breeze creeping through the open window. The walls

Luke James

had a blue flowery pattern which matched the bouquet he had in his hand, giving the whole room a Spring-like feel. It was spacious and the floorboards creaked in a homely way. There was also a clean en-suite bathroom with a large cast iron bath.

Yes, he thought, this place would do just fine. He was already aware of Fury's inner turmoil: even though they were more in-love than ever, despite his mother-in-law's attempts to derail them, their physical intimacy had been waning for some time. He felt responsible. Fury had never turned down his advances, but he couldn't say the same for himself. More and more in recent months, when he'd suspected she was trying to initiate something he'd always managed to find an excuse to do something else - or felt "a headache coming on". Lately, he'd noticed, she'd stopped trying altogether.

Maybe here in Furydale, with him returned to his young self, they could recapture what was missing.

Delicately, he laid the bouquet on the pillow on the left-hand-side of the bed – Fury's side - and began unpacking. He couldn't wait for her to arrive.

He didn't have long before the knock at the door. He opened it and there she stood, glowing like a lake at sunrise. She strutted into the room with a confidence – a determination perhaps – that this was going to be a truly satisfying break away from the real world. He was delighted she seemed to share his mind-set, even without having talked about it. That was a quality of a wonderful life partner. She knew what this meant to him, because it meant the same to her.

She didn't say anything, and weirdly enough she wasn't carrying any bags. Were they outside the door? Had she left them downstairs? He'd happily fetch them for her. She

Model Railway Apocalypse

walked towards him, leaving the door open, and placed her palms on his chest. Then she gripped his shirt and pulled him to her until his lips pressed hard against hers.

It had been a long time since Norman had seen this side of Fury. In fact, he struggled to remember the last time he'd known her act this way - like the horny Helldemon she was. He wondered if he could keep up. What if he disappointed? Would this trip do them more harm than good? He did feel a stirring though, a warming tightness forming in his shaft. She must have felt it too because she stopped kissing him and met his eyes, smiling as if to say: "Well hello."

Then she pushed him onto the bed, climbed on top and kissed him forcefully.

Norman thought they should close the door. But Fury was being so assertive, and this wasn't the real world, so he figured: what the hell? He kissed her neck and let his hands wander up her thighs. Hers were beneath his shirt, moving down his torso. She stroked his ribs with her nails.

He tried to forget the open door but the fear that someone might walk by continued to play on his mind. The more he thought about it, the less comfortable he felt. His hardness waned.

Would getting up and closing the door ruin the mood? This was his wife. She'd want him to feel comfortable, surely?

He glanced at the open doorway and couldn't believe what he saw: Fury standing on the threshold, suitcase in hand and devastation on her face.

Norman looked up at the woman straddling him. It was the barmaid from downstairs. What was she doing on top of him? Hadn't he been kissing his wife? He looked at the

Luke James

door again. Fury was still there. Tears were forming in her red eyes and her skin was flush with demonic blue.

She threw her suitcase at the bed, barely missing Norman's head while he was still pinned beneath the barmaid, who began to cackle. Something, or someone, supernatural was trying to frame him.

Before he could give voice to the notion, Fury vanished.

The barmaid didn't put up a fight as Norman pushed her away and leapt to his feet. Maybe Fury hadn't vanished, but had just run down the corridor. But when he got to the door there was no sign of her. She'd zapped herself out of Furydale.

When he looked back, the barmaid had also vanished. He searched the room and the bathroom, but she wasn't there. He looked inside the wardrobe to see if she was hiding, but there was no sign of her. The window didn't open far enough for anyone to climb through.

There was only one person he knew, other than Fury and Malice, who could change her appearance and vanish. Now that he thought about it, the woman he'd been kissing had tasted a little smoky. That crazed mother-in-law wouldn't go this far, would she? He felt his teeth grind as he realised the truth.

Norman ran down the B&B stairs and out of the pub, into the park. He shouted his wife's name up to the sky, hoping she could hear him. He flung his arms around like a madman in case she could see him.

"Fury!" he called desperately, not knowing if she could hear him. If only he could explain what had happened, that it was his mother-in-law from Hell meddling again! If he could make her understand they could be united again, as they always had been against the malicious bitch!

Model Railway Apocalypse

"Come back! It was your mother kissing me!" he called to the sky. He realised as soon as he'd said it what it must've sounded like to the people around him, who chuckled and pointed fingers, clearly speculating about whether he was insane. But he didn't care. He just wanted his wife to come back so he could explain.

After he'd worn himself out pleading at the sky, it dawned on him: without her he couldn't get back to the real world. He was trapped in Furydale, a prisoner in his own creation.

Luke James

CHAPTER FOUR

Sitting in the armchair beside the spitting fire in The Shaggy Dog, Norman sipped tentatively at a rum and ginger, waiting for something to happen. She'll be back when she's had some time to think. That's what he'd kept telling himself all afternoon.

He checked his watch: 7:57pm - four and a half hours since Fury had left him. It was getting dark out. Did time work in the same way here as in the real world?

Trying to distract himself, he'd spent the afternoon wandering in circles around the town, no longer admiring the living and breathing details of the world brought to life by Fury. He felt as if they were mocking him. The paradise had become his own personal Hell, where he roamed aimlessly, weighed down by chains of guilt and anger and helplessness.

She'll come back soon, he told himself. She must realise it was a mistake.

He stared into the flames, not knowing what else to do.

After walking around the town all afternoon, he'd boarded a train, The Phoenix, at Furydale station. He wondered what would happen. Would the train take him out of Furydale? Would it leave the miniature world and return him to the real one? He knew it was unlikely, but he figured it was worth a shot.

VPredictably, after the train disappeared into the tunnel beneath the hills, it re-emerged at the other end of the tunnel and circled back around into Furydale station. If he

33

Model Railway Apocalypse

had wanted to try going in the other direction he could have crossed the platform and boarded the other train, Jupiter. But instead he stayed put, doing a few more laps on The Phoenix, before feeling sick and returning to The Shaggy Dog for another drink.

At the bar the barmaid didn't act as though anything unusual had taken place, confirming his suspicions: she had nothing to do with this mess. Queasiness tugged at his insides each time he thought about his mother-in-law's tongue in his throat. The thought still haunted him while he drank his fourth 'Stormy Sea', not knowing whether it was the drink or the violation making him feel ill.

More likely, it was the knowledge that Fury was out there somewhere, hurting. It was nothing new to her. She'd endured a lot to be with him: the outrage from her mother; the ominous silence from her father, who now acted as if she'd never existed. He could never understand why she'd given it all up for him. He wasn't special. But the way she told it: he was some kind of exotic curiosity.

VShe'd looked human when they met. It was only after a year that she revealed her "true" self. Far from being horrified, he was overwhelmed and excited. Even as a human, she'd been an exotic curiosity to him too. By the time he knew the truth, he'd already fallen for her.

He'd learnt early on not to ask too many questions about her past. She was guarded and he accepted that. He still didn't fully understand why she chose him. Best not to question that too much either. Or the fact that one day he'd die and she'd go on without him. Would she still think of him in 1000 years time?

"Say buddy, you all right?" a friendly country accent asked. It was the merry patron he'd added to the model town as he'd completed it. A large man with a baby-face,

Luke James

he was sitting at a nearby table. True to his design he was holding a half-full pint glass.

"Fine," Norman replied, stirred out of his contemplation. He swallowed the last of his Stormy Sea. Exhausted, he went back to the room he'd booked for Fury and himself. Maybe Fury would come back for him. Or maybe he would wake up back in the real world.

While brushing his teeth, he caught his reflection in the bathroom mirror. His tired, aged face stared back. The image blurred as tears pooled in his eyes.

Fury had stormed out of the spare room slamming the door behind her. She paced around the house, but everything reminded her of Norman, so she went out. It was only after several alarmed reactions from passers-by she realised she'd relapsed into her demon skin. Embarrassed, she reluctantly returned to her human appearance. She missed how powerful she felt as a demon. Being human made her tired.

She hadn't planned on walking into town, but that's where her feet took her. It was better than being at home. She went straight to the bakery and bought some Chocolate Fudge cake. Chocolate was one of the things she loved about Earth. After gorging on cake she went straight to the nearest bar, where she stayed for the next few hours, getting more and more tanked on red wine while pondering her life choices.

Had her mother been right about Norman? Was he really just a "wretched" mortal? Seeing him grind against another woman had thrown everything into question. He had created the foul barmaid, and now he thought he could do what he liked with her!

She shouldn't have been surprised; like God, humans

Model Railway Apocalypse

were arrogant. Why wouldn't he flirt with his own creation? The difference was God, if he stuck around long enough, could crush humans. She'd become too human. She'd let Norman play God. And now he'd crushed her. The demon in her couldn't let that stand.

Even though home was a ten minute walk from town, she was in no state to make the journey on foot, so she hailed a taxi. The driver tried to make conversation, commenting on how a woman like her shouldn't be out on her own, and how men couldn't be trusted – as if she didn't already know! It seemed to Fury that he didn't mean it as a condemnation, but rather as an excuse for men's behaviour, as he eyed her up in the rear-view mirror all the way home. She tried to ignore him as he chatted on about his other job as a guitarist in a rock band. She replied with the occasional "I see" and "Oh right", but after he didn't get the hint, she snapped.

"Just drive the fucking taxi, mortal!" she shouted, exploding into her full demon form.

The driver shrieked and swerved across the road, hitting a streetlight. He flung open the driver's door. Fury was thrown forward by the impact, her horns impaling the driver's headrest. Her irritation was quickly replaced by amusement as she watched the driver try to throw himself out of the car without undoing his seatbelt first. He fumbled clumsily with his buckle, yelping to himself, before finally escaping the taxi and running screaming into the night.

Fury climbed forwards into the driver's seat and drove herself home in the limping wreck. Feeling generous, she didn't even charge herself.

Luke James

It was nearly 11pm by the time she got home. Once through the front door, she relaxed into her demonic state. She stumbled up the stairs, making her way to the spare room. She was surprised to see the LED lights were still on inside the small buildings and the fairground rides were still lit up and alive. The trains circled the town, in and out of tunnels and over bridges. Somewhere in there was Norman. There was no way he could leave without her.

Without much difficulty, she found the switch to turn off the trains. One of them stopped dead, halfway into the tunnel, the other in the station. There was a train depot set away from the town where they were probably supposed to go, but she didn't care. She could do what she liked.

It dawned on her the kind of power she now had over her husband. He'd built this model world. She'd brought it to life and he'd thought he was God. But now he was banished, trapped inside his creation. Fury couldn't help but smirk; there was a new God in town.

When she thought about what she'd given up for him, the fire inside made her claws grow like supercharged black shoots, sprouting from her blue fingers. Letting her anger flow through her arms, she dragged her talons over the surface of the model world, carving deep valleys into the landscape. She tightened both hands into fists and raised them above her head.

Demonic instincts returned like an old friend. She brought her knuckles down with all her rage.

The world shook - the model one, and the room.

The surface around her fists cracked. The fairground Ferris wheel collapsed, landing on the carousel. The train track was still intact, and so were the buildings, but a large crack stretched halfway across the surface.

Making the world shake was satisfying. She raised her

Model Railway Apocalypse

fists to do it again.

Screams shook Norman from his sleep. Looking around through sleep-heavy eyes, he tried to figure out what had woken him. It took him a few moments to recognise where he was. Dizziness set in as he recalled how he came to be there, on his own. The bedside lamp rattled. Screams came through the window and the corridor. He got up to investigate, but the world shuddered violently and he lost his footing, falling back onto the bed.

Maybe I shouldn't have had so much to drink, he thought.

"Earthquake!" a nearby voice called, as dust floated down from the ceiling. Norman climbed out of bed.

"Earthquake! Get out of the building!" the voice came again.

The lights flickered as Norman put on his shoes and a flannel robe. He ran out of the room and down the corridor.

Descending the stairs with the earth shaking wasn't easy. Half way down the narrow stairway a great weight thumped on his back, sending him hurtling the rest of the way.

Lying on his front at the bottom of the stairs, his arms and legs throbbed. His forehead felt sticky-warm. Before he could think about standing up, a large arm grabbed him and lifted him to his feet.

"There you go buddy. Can't lie around here all day."

VNorman's eyes focused on the source of the voice. It was the large, baby-faced man who'd spoken to him in the pub earlier that night. He still held a pint of stout in one hand, while propping Norman up with the other.

They were surrounded by panicked guests, all battling to find their way out of the building while the ground trembled beneath their feet and plaster rained down on their heads.

Luke James

Outside, Norman and the large man joined the crowd gathering on the edge of the park. Now they could hear the thunderous banging which accompanied the shuddering earth, as though the moon had fallen from its cord and was bouncing towards them.

"Are you okay, buddy?" the man who'd helped him asked. "You had quite a fall."

Norman was able to get a closer look at him now: he was in his forties, wore an ill-fitting shirt and had a stupidly big grin on his face.

The earth finally stopped shaking. After a few moments of silence and stillness, everyone sighed in relief.

"I'm okay, thank you," Norman replied.

The large man offered his hand.

"Barry," he said. "Pleased to meet you. You can call me Baz."

"Norman." He shook Baz's hand. "But only my wife calls me Norm."

"Sounds like a real ballbuster," Baz scoffed.

This is her doing, Norman thought with a sinking feeling. She's taking out her anger.

Without warning, The Shaggy Dog launched into their air. It shot up one hundred feet before stopping dead above their heads. The crowd gasped, collectively craning their necks as they watched the three-storey building floating in the sky. Through hollow floors they could see up into the bar. Bottles fell, shattering like raindrops when they met the earth. Exposed wires and pipes jutted out of the ground, flickering and sparking. The basement, beer barrels and all, was exposed.

Then, like some kind of nightmare theme park ride, the building came crashing down. It disintegrated instantly on impact. The crowd ducked as debris flew over them.

Model Railway Apocalypse

When the air cleared The Shaggy Dog was no more than a crater surrounded by rubble.

Norman raised his eyebrows in alarm. "Ballbuster indeed," he agreed. Baz puffed his cheeks, bemused.

Luke James

CHAPTER FIVE

Still in his flannel robe and pyjamas, Norman had resigned himself to lying on a bench in the park. He'd been there all night, and now he watched the dawn break, fascinated. Somehow there was this magical sky above him and not, as might be expected, the spare room ceiling. He might have designed the landscape, but the sky was all Fury. That was why it was so darkly beautiful. He couldn't see her, but he knew she was up there somewhere.

The horizon too was Fury's handiwork. He suspected that if he tried walking towards it, it would be like the background of an old video game, where he'd never get any closer, no matter how far he travelled. Would he, sooner or later, reach the edge of the world? Could he fall off? What would happen to him if he did?

"No aftershocks then," Baz said, lying on the adjacent bench. He'd latched on to Norman, who didn't fancy bundling into the town hall or the church with the rest of the locals. They seemed to be the strongest structures in the town. Most of the buildings appeared to have held together, except for The Shaggy Dog, which had been annihilated. The shaken townsfolk, traumatised by the sight of an entire building launching into the air Wizard-of-Oz style, were taking comfort in each other.

"What do you think lifted The Dog like that?" Baz asked. He was still holding an empty stout glass in his hand. "I've never seen anything like it."

"I don't know," Norman said. But of course he did. Perhaps

41

Model Railway Apocalypse

misguidedly, he felt reassured in his understanding of what had happened. Fury had lost her temper and taken it out on the model world. It had gone quiet since. Obviously she hadn't been in a sound state of mind. But she was a rational woman. Once she'd had a chance to cool down she'd be back to her sensible self, and she'd return to listen to his version of events. Then they could go back to the real world together, laughing about the misunderstanding.

Fury's awesome display of power had astounded him. She wasn't missing any passion when she'd thrown that building. Her past had always intrigued him – or rather the idea of her past. He knew it shouldn't, and he'd never told her as much, but it turned him on.

Now, she was up there somewhere, master of his world, making the ground shake and buildings fly. That was a pretty sexy thought..

Sunlight broke through the open curtains, waking Fury from her awkward slumber on the spare room floor. She couldn't remember falling asleep.

Perching at eye level, she observed the miniature chaos through sleepy eyes. Her head was heavy. She rubbed her eyes and winced as she noticed the nasty gashes and grazes on her knuckles and the sides of her hands.

When she stood up and went to the kitchen heavy black clouds still hung over her vision. She made coffee, staring into the steam pouring out of the kettle as it reached boiling point. She over-filled the mug until scorching water spilled all over the kitchen worktop. Unfazed, she gripped the mug tightly between two hands and carried it back to the spare room, stopping briefly when she caught the reflection in the hallway mirror.

Her long dark hair hung over her muscular blue skin,

42

Luke James

which was dressed in strips of morning sunlight from the landing window. Her crimson eyes, which always looked larger in her demon form, had a luminescence about them, telling stories of a fiercer, darker world wrapped around this one. She slipped off the dress she'd slept in and smiled at herself, as though acknowledging an old friend. She looked both youthful and ancient, beautiful and monstrous.

Returning to the spare room, she surveyed the miniature world. Norman was still in there, somewhere. She smirked as she recalled smashing up The Shaggy Dog.

But for a flicker of a moment, her smile faltered as she considered the possibility that he'd been inside when she'd throttled it. Could she have killed him?

No. She squinted at the model world; her attention was drawn to a small patch of the park which was faintly illuminated.

When she opened her eyes again the luminosity faded. Once more, she squinted and there it was. She knew it was Norman. He was alive in there, survived to endure another day. And what a day she had planned.

She produced a lighter retrieved from the kitchen drawer and lowered it towards the model world.

For the second time in a few hours, Norman woke to screaming. He sat bolt upright on the bench, saddened he wasn't waking up to Fury offering him a chance to explain his version of events.

He smelled burning bread. He glanced across the road and saw the bakery wrapped in flames.

"Jesus Christ!" Baz yelled. Norman had forgotten he was there.

"I hope everyone got out."

Model Railway Apocalypse

Regardless, the fire was too far gone for anyone to do anything about it. Norman hadn't installed a fire station so there was no one to fight the flames. If it continued, the fire would spread to the florist, and maybe even the general store.

Norman was hit by the notion that the whole model railway would go up in flames - it was built on plywood.

Fury wouldn't let him burn, surely?

This might be his only chance. Norman leapt up and ran across the road.

"What you doing?" Baz called after him.

Skipping over the cracks left by the quake, Norman ran into the florist. There was no one inside. He looked around at the range of flowers, which were stored in buckets. There were lilies, violets, roses and geraniums, none of them would do.

"Get out of there. You're a lunatic!" Baz shouted from the street outside.

Norman scanned the arrangements, determined to get what he came for. It was sensory overload. There were so many colours. But there was just one colour and one type of flower he was looking for. The walls caught fire around him. Smoke poured into the room.

Finally he saw it: a bucket of hyacinths – and they had purple! He couldn't believe his luck.

He grabbed all the purple hyacinths in the bucket and ran out of the florist, as the whole display went up in flames.

"What the bleedin' hell's wrong with you?" Baz demanded. "You went in there to get flowers?"

"Not just any flower," Norman said, sniffing the bunch in his hands. "Purple hyacinths."

"Your wife's favourite?"

Luke James

"No. Purple hyacinths have a special meaning. They say: 'Please forgive me.'"

They watched the florist collapse in the flames that had consumed the bakery.

Baz shook his head, exasperated. "Mate, you must seriously have pissed off your wife."

He has no idea, Norman thought to himself.

"Bloody shame though," Baz cursed. "I was gonna get breakfast from the bakery."

"Maybe they'll still do toast," Norman said.

Without warning, it started to rain heavily on the town. In a few seconds, the fire was out.

There was an agonised shriek a few meters away. It came from a man wearing a striped apron. Norman figured it was the baker, grieving for his demolished business. But it seemed more intense than grief. And he kept going, shrieking and calling out, flapping his arms around.

"It burns!" he cried. "It's burning!"

"No. It's over. The fires out," someone nearby reassured him.

The baker still jumped around, frenzied.

"No! Not the fire…the rain!"

Others began to notice it too. The dark rain was indeed burning. Norman's skin itched. He rubbed it with his sleeve but it didn't seem to help. It was starting to peel. He glanced again at the baker, who was now on his knees, crying out to the heavens.

The smell of coffee filled the air as the crowd ran back to the town hall to take shelter from the burning rain.

Fury emptied her cup onto the fire before it got out of control and destroyed the whole model. She didn't want it to be over too quickly. Killing wasn't her art form; the

Model Railway Apocalypse

damned souls delivered to her in Hell were already dead. Her job, and her pleasure, had been to deliver epiphanies – the kind that left an eternal stain.

She'd been out of the game for too long. Her creativity had dwindled through lack of practice. Starting small seemed appropriate. She closed the curtains in the spare room, blocking out the daylight. The LED lights were still on in the remaining buildings, so she turned them off, casting the world into darkness. She flicked the spare room lights on and off quickly several times, amused by the effect it must be having in the miniature realm.

She couldn't see the people living out their lives – or trying to - just the elusive glow signalling Norma's location. She couldn't directly control the influence of the elements she added or changed, any more than one could control the diaspora of chemicals stirred into a cauldron. But she could meddle with the spirit of the world, poisoning its essence with her own designs. Just a few tweaks could transform the fantasyland into a nightmare for those inside.

It seemed ironic to her. She'd used powers meant for torturing to bring joy to her husband. But now she was using them to torture him after all.

Norman's workbench was in the corner of the room. She rummaged through the drawers and found lots of goodies: pens, paints, modelling materials and more track. There were some boxes tucked beneath the workbench. She investigated their contents.

Luke James

CHAPTER SIX

With sore skin, Norman and Baz walked through the abandoned fairground, taking in the destruction left by the quake and the burning rain. The townsfolk had become aimless after their successive ordeals, no longer going about their lives with any sense of order or purpose, but wandering around like zombies. An increasingly large crowd gathered around a priest who was delivering a sermon in the corner of the park. A doom-sayer held up a sign saying: "Repent, sinners. Repent."

Then the eclipse came.

Daylight narrowed to a single slit in the sky before disappearing completely. There were more gasps from the locals. At least the lights were still on inside the surviving buildings. Figuring it was safer than roaming through the chaos without any light, Norman and Baz headed to the general store which, thanks to the rain, had survived the fire before it spread from the now ruined florist. Norman tucked the bunch of violet hyacinths into the deep pocket of his robe, determined to deliver them safely to Fury the first chance he got.

As they crossed the cracked road, every light in the world went out.

"Damn," Baz said.

"Mmm," Norman agreed. His eyes ached as his pupils dilated, straining to see

"If there's a God in this place," Baz said, "somebody has really pissed him off."

Model Railway Apocalypse

There were several flashes of lightning. Norman's corneas felt as though they were burning. He closed his eyes.

After a few seconds the lightning stopped, and he reopened them.

"Ouch," Baz muttered, rubbing his eyes.

They stood in the utter darkness, bewildered. It dawned on Norman that he was now resident in a world where his angry demon wife was God. Maybe he'd tempted fate by calling the town 'Furydale.'

Baz still clutched the empty pint glass in his hand. With The Shaggy Dog gone, the general store was the only place they could get a drink. Norman had never been a big drinker, but right now it seemed like a good idea. Plus he could use some food.

"Hello?" they called, once inside. But there was no answer. No one else had dared go near any buildings since the fire and the earthquake. They couldn't see a thing, but they felt their way along the shelves.

Norman had a real craving for a Danish pastry. He fumbled his way along one of the aisles, identifying each item he came across. He found the cereal first, then the condiments, then the bread. The pastries must be around here somewhere. He reached the end of the aisle and turned the corner.

There was a clatter and a smashing of glass in the next aisle, followed by a muttered apology. Baz had found the alcohol section. Quick work, Norman thought.

He reached out to the shelves at the end of the aisle and felt the soft plastic packaging of a four-pack of pastries. He ripped it open and stuffed the first one into his mouth, enjoying the comforting taste of cinnamon mixed with moist pastry and icing sugar.

In the next aisle a bottle cap fell to the floor as Baz

refilled his beer mug.

Norman was tucking into his second pastry when blinding daylight came flooding in and screams rang from outside.

They rushed out of the general store. Through squinted eyes they saw townsfolk darting around like ants from a disturbed nest. Among them, petrified faces gaped at the skyline behind where Norman and Baz were standing. Before they could turn around to see what had earned such a response, a large shadow fell over the dispersing crowd.

A tractor spun through the air, soaring over the rooftops.

It crashed down in the park, shattering on impact. Shrapnel flew everywhere, several pieces embedding themselves in people unfortunate enough to get in the way.

One tractor wheel remained intact and bounced after the fleeing crowd. It changed direction erratically, leaving the scattering crowd unsure where to run. Eventually it smashed through a park bench and landed in the duck pond, sending ducks flapping frantically into the air. Well-rehearsed at impromptu flight, they swiftly assembled into formation, putting the fleeing humans to shame. A cacophony of quacks flew across the sky, towards the hills.

Now everyone saw what had thrown the tractor.

Norman's feet rooted to the spot, while Baz glugged down the contents of his beer mug. Locals mindlessly sprinted in circles, shocked and aimless.

Striding over the hills towards them was a fifty foot tall naked woman.

The panicked townsfolk watched in disbelief as the giant woman picked up steamtrain, raised it above her head

Model Railway Apocalypse

and lugged it towards the town. It landed on the church, crushing the tall spire like a bowling ball hitting an ice cream cone. Grey brickwork flew everywhere.

As she got closer, with her nippleless breasts and sealed crotch, Norman recognised her as Dinahdoll – a memento from Malice's childhood. It seemed Fury had discovered the containers he'd tucked away beneath his workbench; some of Malice's old toys, some of his. His chest tightened as a Pandora's box of nightmarish possibilities snapped open in his mind.

Tanned skin, green eyes, brunette and slightly curvy, Dinahdoll was the progressives' answer to Barbie. The toy company always intended her to be on the larger side, in an effort to reduce body-image related eating disorders among young girls. Now she was the size of a tower block.

Her long dark hair danced in the air behind her as she moved swiftly and gracefully, covering the distance from the hills to the town in just a few strides. She flattened the post office with a single step. The crowd scattered like spilled M&Ms as the building crumbled beneath her foot, rubble flying everywhere.

Norman and Baz ran to the far side of the park and ducked beneath a hedgerow, as if it could offer any protection from the rampaging giantess.

She stood in the road. It cracked under her weight. With hands on hips, she studied the little people, watching with a satisfied smile as they scurried back and forth trying to find somewhere to hide.

Only the priest who'd been delivering the sermon in the park stood firm. He looked up at her, waving his Bible around and shouting.

"Leave this place, you unGodly demon! You unholy wench!"

Luke James

Norman watched her face. He tried to decipher the significance of her presence – what did it tell him about his wife's mindset? Her sadistic games were becoming a rather more than a petty reaction to a misunderstanding. Was this the price for marrying a Helldemon? He fought back the idea that this was the "real" Fury.

The giantess smirked at the priest. Then she stepped on him.

The screaming locals discovered a new pitch.

"Jesus! Do you think she's the one behind the earthquakes and the power outage?" Baz asked.

It took a few moments for Norman to detach what Baz meant by "she" – the giantess – and "she" his wife. They were the same thing.

"If I had to guess, I'd say they were connected," Norman replied.

Dinah Doll picked up a bus as it drove into town, oblivious to the disturbances. By the time the driver and passengers noticed what was going on, they were being held high above the rooftops, swung around in perfect terror while the giantess laughed.

Norman and Baz and the others watched, helpless as she placed the bus back down on the road, then booted it down the street as though taking a penalty kick. It burst through a fence and descended into the river valley.

"Run, insects!" she shrieked, her voice deep and croaky.

She stepped into the park and raised her arms up into a posture that resembled one half of a pair of ballroom dancers. She stood up on the balls of her feet and pranced forwards and backwards and in circles around the park while people desperately dodged her footfalls. Her wicked waltz proved fatal to those who weren't quick enough. She crushed them underfoot, bones turning to paste and guts

Model Railway Apocalypse

spilling. Every so often she'd add a little backwards flick of her foot, deliberately kicking some poor soul through the air.

Norman and Baz watched the whole thing from behind the hedgerow.

"This is terrible!" Baz cried. "We have to do something!"

Subdued and appalled by the violence, Norman had no intention of doing anything other than surviving long enough to explain himself to his wife. He still had the purple hyacinths tucked into the pocket of his robe, determined to give them to her the first chance he got; if only he could survive this madness. The people around him were suffering, but Norman wasn't sure how real they were. Were they alive? Or were they a simulation of life?

Baz gasped in horror. To him, this world was real, with real people who were really dying in pain and anguish.

"Over there. Look!" he said, pointing at an attractive woman in a summer dress, who was desperately screaming while running back and forth beneath Dinahdoll's flouncing toes, trying to avoid getting squished.

"We have to help her!" Baz said, launching over the hedgerow and running towards the woman.

Norman didn't know if he was just being cynical when it occurred to him that Baz might not be charging to the rescue if the woman wasn't so attractive. After all, there were others in the same position.

He remained behind the hedgerow, watching curiously while Baz darted across the park, calling out to the woman in the summer dress. The large man was surprisingly spritely as he ducked and leapt out of the way of the enormous dancing feet. He certainly moved more gracefully than the naked behemoth terrorising the town. Norman noticed he'd even left his beer mug behind. He

Luke James

must have been serious about rescuing this woman.

As Baz reached her he tripped on a piece of tractor and fell flat on his face. He rolled onto his back as a colossal foot came down on top of him.

Norman felt his jaw clench as Baz disappeared beneath her.

When the foot lifted up, he saw that the large man had narrowly rolled out of the way. Baz jumped up quickly and leapt onto the giant foot as it swooshed through the air, still practising its dance routine. He clung on to her like a spider.

The giantess halted her prancing. She kicked out, trying to rid herself of the human parasite. But he held on tightly to the top of her foot.

She kicked again, and again, but the determined Baz didn't budge. He slowly shuffled towards her ankle, which he wrapped his limbs around like a tree-hugger, strengthening his grip. No matter how much she shook her foot she couldn't lose him.

A horrified crowd formed, watching on. Even the woman Baz had set out to rescue in the first place stood gawking in disbelief.

Although he was distracting the giantess from terrorising the poor townsfolk, the fallout damage to the already broken fairground was still devastating, as she flapped around trying to get rid of him. She kicked over an ice-cream van, unrooted trees and stamped on unfortunate onlookers.

Baz was shuffling bear-like up her leg. Norman couldn't help but admire his determination and skill. With his ripped shirt and bloodied face he was like a portly action hero.

Visibly irritated, Dinahdoll reached down to scratch off

Model Railway Apocalypse

the unlikely action hero. But Baz saw his opportunity and shifted his grip from her legs to her fingers. He clung to her knuckles, doing well to avoid being crushed like an insect in her palm.

She raised him to eye level and inspected him as he straddled her middle finger. The irritation faded from her face. She seemed almost amused by him.

Baz crawled onto the back of her hand. He sprang to his feet and ran swiftly along the length of her arm, finding the bulge of her shoulder.

She reached her other hand up to brush him off.

Norman braced himself, expecting to see his new companion plummet to his death, but Baz - now straddling her shoulder blade - leant forwards and grabbed her earlobe.

Was he whispering in her ear? Like a little devil?

She stood still. A sudden uneasy calm took hold of the town. People watched, waiting for something horrible to happen. Would he fall off? Would she squash him like a bug? Would she peel him off and throw him over the hills and far away? They watched in fearful anticipation.

Without warning, Dinahdoll giggled. It wasn't the cackle that had gone with her bullying and maiming of the locals. It was a joyful chuckle, almost endearing. What had he said to her? She angled her ear towards him to listen some more, the smile on her face growing wider still.

Norman, cowering behind the hedge, could just about make out a grin on Baz's face. He looked alarmingly relaxed.

The crowd murmured as Dinahdoll raised her hand up to her shoulder. But instead of squashing or throwing the large little man, she shaped her palm into a cradle, into which Baz leapt. She wrapped her fingers around him, and

Luke James

brought his head to her mouth.

There was a collective gasp. Norman cringed, unsure if he'd ever recover from seeing a man's head bitten off in the cold light of day.

But no such horror occurred. She merely pursed her lips and gently kissed him on the head.

Comfortably clutched in her fingers, Baz stuck his arm out and gave the onlookers a thumbs-up.

There was cheering and applause all around.

Then the soldiers and the tanks rolled in, all guns blazing.

Luke James

CHAPTER SEVEN

The giant woman swayed and groaned as wounds appeared all over her body. Rockets and bullets flew at her like kamikaze bees, blood bursting from the injuries left by their devastating stings. It was almost heart-breaking to watch as she staggered back and forth, trying to balance herself while her flesh rippled under the onslaught. She still clutched Baz tightly in her hand, holding him high above her head, away from the projectile. He wriggled and yelped like a demented hamster, arms and legs flapping around in the air. The townsfolk scattered.

Norman recognised his old army figures and tanks: four vehicles and twenty on foot. They'd been in the same box as Malice's Dinahdoll. His Uncle, who'd been in the Army, had given them to him when he was a child. Norman had forgotten all about them. His uncle had acted as if he was still on the battlefield during Christmas dinners and birthday parties. It never really inspired Norman to play war with the toys.

Hearing the shouts from Baz over the noise of the artillery, Norman couldn't let it go on - not with his friend up there in the firing line.

Leaping over the hedgerow, he ran towards the gathering militia. Safely out of the firing line, which was directed firmly into the sky, he approached one of the tanks. While he'd never really played with the toy soldiers, he knew enough to tell which one was in charge. He called

Model Railway Apocalypse

out to a lean silver-haired man, whose head poked out the top of the monstrous vehicle.

The soldier couldn't hear him over the gunfire. Norman thrashed his arms around to get his attention. Eventually it worked, but the military man simply waved him aside.

There were calls from several of the military men and the gunfire ceased. Norman turned around to see Dinahdoll descending towards them.

Full of bullets and now bloodless, she fell like a ragdoll, landing just shy of Norman and the militia. The ground rumbled for seconds afterwards.

There was no sign of Baz.

The military men raised their guns in the air and cheered.

Norman didn't expect to care so much about the fate of his new companion. He ran over to the fallen giantess, searching frantically for any sign the large man may have survived. Had the artillery fire somehow missed him? Had he leapt free in the fall?

Norman called out Baz's name, which took him by surprise. Back in the real world, most of his attention had been devoted to his family, and his hobbies - which were by no coincidence, mostly solitary activities. Friends had never been high on Norman's priority list. He preferred to keep himself to himself.

Somehow Baz, in his childlike decency and earnestness, had won him over.

There was no sign of his body. Norman could only conclude that he had been crushed.

His heart raced as he felt a surge of anger. Behind him the military men still cheered. He never had liked army-types.

Luke James

"Fools!" he shouted, catching the eye of the silver-haired man in charge.

The soldiers halted their celebrations and gave Norman a dirty look. He was still in his robe with the hyacinths tucked into his pocket.

"You roll into town in your tin-cans, guns-a-blazing! Do you even look where you're shooting?"

The soldiers laughed. The silver-haired man climbed down from his tank.

"We just saved this town from that big ugly bitch. You should be thanking us."

"I'll thank you when you climb back into your sardine-tin and fuck off!" Norman said, pointing down the street.

The soldiers goaded him with howls.

"I don't like your tone, son," the leader said.

"I don't like your breath." Norman waved his hand in front of his face.

There were "oooo"s and "errr"s from the soldiers.

"Those flowers for me?" the leader asked.

"Yeah," Norman answered. "Bend over and I'll give them to you."

The soldiers laughed. The silver-haired man snorted along with them. Then he punched Norman in the jaw.

As Norman collapsed to the ground, cradling his face, there were more cheers.

"I'm Major Pierce. I lead these men. This town belongs to us now."

"I preferred when it belonged to the giant naked woman," Norman spat.

He heard a wheezing noise coming from behind him. The woman's cleavage wobbled and rippled, as though each breast was somehow alive. Then a head poked out between them.

Model Railway Apocalypse

"Baz!" Norman rushed over to him as he wriggled and writhed his way out like a butterfly from a cocoon. It was awkward to watch. He gasped for air. Norman was so distracted by the uncomfortable spectacle that he was delayed in offering his hand. He helped pull Baz from the fleshy incarceration. His grateful companion slid out and thumped on the floor, clumsily pulling Norman down on top of him.

The soldiers laughed.

"Get a room, boys!" Major Pierce teased.

Ferocity was a spider again. From the wall she watched her daughter, pleased to see her getting back to her old self. She was even wearing her old armour, forged in the fires of Hell, given to her at birth. The moment when demons grew into their birthright was a ceremonious occasion, like a birthday. Ferocity could remember her daughter's Armour Day well, even if it was eight-hundred years ago. How luminous she was. How fearsome. How all the other demon mothers looked on with envy.

Now, Fury was embracing her inner demoness again. Ferocity fought back the temptation to appear to her daughter, desperate to hold her the way she used to, but fearful that an altercation might drive her back to the pitiable husband. For now she would just have to watch, admiring her daughter's creativity in tormenting the tedious human. She smiled at the ingenious way Fury interfered with the miniature world - sculpting and crafting, mixing elements together. The artist had returned.

Fury was concentrating hard. She had been moving figures around. Ferocity watched with glee as she went to the workbench, pulled out tools, rummaged among boxes,

Luke James

mixed paint. Now she seemed to be carving a hole in the top of a hill.

Keeping a distance at this point might cause her daughter to draw an unfortunate connection between the betrayal of her husband and her mother's absence, but she hoped not. Perhaps keeping away from her daughter during this crucial time would allow her the opportunity to crave maternal comfort, making herself all the more welcome when she did return.

She would just make some excuse for not coming today, lockdown in Hell or something like that – they were frequent enough to be believable, usually when some reckless soul had escaped their pit.

No amount of coaxing could draw out of Baz what he'd whispered into the ear of the giantess during his heroic moments before the soldiers arrived. They sat by the pond in the corner of the park, dangling their feet over the edge. The ducks still hadn't returned – the tractor wheel must have sunk to the bottom.

A jauntiness had taken over Norman since his new friend squirmed his way out of the protective cleavage. The relief had relegated the depression over his persistent ill-fortune to the back of his mind... for now.

"Come on," Norman prodded. "That's got to be one mighty chat-up line. What did you say to her?"

"You're too young!" Baz quipped.

"I'm at least two decades your senior," Norman said.

Baz chuckled, though it felt a little strained as he looked down at his feet.

"In that case, you're too old!"

"Damn you!"

"I wouldn't want to give you a heart attack or anything."

Model Railway Apocalypse

"With a jump of two decades I could tell you a thing or two," Norman said, crossing his arms.

"Oh yeah, I meant to ask about your wife."

The melancholy returned like a wasp to a picnic; he saw flashes of Fury standing in that doorway, pain on her face.

"What about her?" Norman hesitated.

"Where is she? What have you done to upset her?"

That wasn't really the question Norman wanted to answer. It still hadn't really set in - the giantess, the soldiers, the chaos – it was all Fury. The world they'd first visited was built upon his imagination. But this wasn't him anymore. Now it was all her. He was choking on the fumes of her mind, her anger. Misguided anger. How could she think he'd do that to her? Couldn't she tell? Didn't she know him better than that?

The more he thought about it, the hotter the flame of injustice burned.

"A misunderstanding," he finally answered.

"That's okay. You don't want to talk about it."

"No, it's okay."

"Well, how did you meet?"

Now that was a slightly easier question to answer, and Baz needed the distraction from his recent ordeal.

"Otherworldly forces," Norman answered with a smile.

Luke James

CHAPTER EIGHT

"I was out one night. Just got into photography so I was trying to learn how to take night time shots. Everything and anything I found, I snapped it. You couldn't say I lived in the most exciting or interesting town, but I'd read somewhere: your subject doesn't have to be interesting, just captured in an interesting way. There were loads of multi-storey car parks in my town. During the day they were your regular soulless concrete blocks. But at night time they were always lit up like something out of a science-fiction story, illuminated grids like the inside of a computer or a cagey government facility.

"I probably sound a bit crazy, but I was doing anything I could to occupy my mind. My dad had just died. Mum had gone only two years earlier. Work wasn't great and I was sliding down a scary path. They called it "depression", but that sounds too clinical. Sadness is what it was - this haunting, tugging feeling of heaviness, like lying in a bath while the water runs out. Like nothing was really worth it.

"The camera was my father's. I'd found it while sorting through his things. I must have taken over a hundred photos in the space of half an hour that evening, walking around, camping out across the road to a multi-storey. I'd got long shots and close ups and all the angles, playing around with the exposure to give the tungsten lights that supernatural glow. I snapped some passing drunks and a roaming fox...

"Just as my battery ran out, she appeared. I hadn't

Model Railway Apocalypse

noticed her coming until she was a few feet away, walking along the pavement directly towards me, wearing what I can only describe as a Warrior Princess costume. Skimpy armour, broad at the shoulders, tight at the thighs, cleavage cosseted between silver breastplates - more for aesthetic than actual protection.

"At first I thought I'd been reading too many fantasy novels, or someone had slipped something in my drink. But would a hallucination have been shivering like she did? Would a trick of the mind have been able to wear my jacket as I walked her home?

"I figured she was on her way home from a costume party. She didn't say anything to suggest otherwise. In fact, she didn't say much at all. She just stopped and stood about a meter away from me, smiling and shivering. She didn't say anything about where she lived - not even after I asked – so I walked her back to my place. I figured she'd fill in all the blanks when she wanted too. I found her some warm clothes – a hoodie and trackie-bottoms. She was demure, reserved, and elegant. I made her a hot drink – chocolate, I think. She sipped it as if it was the first time she'd ever tasted it. She said she'd come from far away. A very hot place I wouldn't know.

"She never showed any intention of leaving. The whole thing was unfathomable. You have to understand, I was scraping along the bottom of sanity when she appeared. So I just accepted it. My life was empty, then this otherworldly woman appeared. It became my very purpose to take care of her. It was like she had come just for me. Like she had her ear pressed up against a dimensional wall. That's what I still believe."

Luke James

"Why don't you just call her?" Baz asked.

Norman smirked as though it was a ridiculous idea. Like that would work. But after considering it for a moment, it didn't seem so bad. Would it work? He didn't understand the physics of magic. But it had to be worth a try. If he could find a phone in town and dial his home number, would she pick up?

He leapt up and grabbed Baz, who was alarmed by his sudden movement, by the shoulders.

"You're a genius!"

"Well, I thought it might be kind of obvious. I assumed you'd tried it already."

Screams came from across the park. A woman was running away from the town hall, chased by a soldier. It was the woman Baz had tried to rescue, before he tripped and ended up seducing the giantess. She was coming towards them, her dress torn and her shoulder exposed.

"Help me!" she screamed.

The soldier chasing her was laughing, clearly relishing her terror. He was topless and had a bottle of booze in his hand.

Fucking soldiers, Norman thought. He grabbed Baz by the shoulder and pulled him down to hide behind the hedgerow.

"Are you going to hide behind hedgerows your entire life?" Baz asked.

"Shut up and grab her."

The girl ran past the hedgerow into the clearing by the pond. Baz did as Norman said, pulling her down behind the hedgerow with them. He held his hand over her mouth to stop her from screaming.

Norman pressed his finger to his lips, indicating for her to be quiet. She nodded. Baz pulled his hand away.

65

Model Railway Apocalypse

"Where did you go girl?" The soldier taunted. "I'm comin' after you!"

Norman stuck his leg out as the soldier ran into the clearing. He fell forwards and landed on his face by the edge of the pond.

"Sonovabitch!" he shouted.

Baz jumped on the fallen grunt and pinned him down. The soldier struggled and reached for his gun. Norman beat him to it. He cocked it and pointed it at the man.

"Let him up, Baz," Norman said.

Baz stood up, followed by the sheepish soldier.

"What are you boys playin' at? Haven't you heard we run this town now?"

"Haven't you heard of decency?" Norman replied. He threw the gun into the pond.

"Sonovabitch!" the soldier shouted.

He turned and waded into the pond to fetch the weapon. Norman, Baz and the girl watched him. It was a large pond. Did he really think he could find it? Would it still work?

"You jus' wait 'til I find my gun. I'm gonna mess you boys up."

The surface rippled and the soldier let out a grunt, jerking in the water.

"The fuck was that?"

"Look!" the girl said, quietly pointing to some ripples in the water a short distance from the soldier.

Norman and Baz both saw it, only fleetingly, before it disappeared beneath the surface. It was a large fin.

"Oh my days," Baz muttered. Then louder, he said: "Oi, buddy. You might want to get out now."

"You shut the hell up, fat man. I'm gonna shoot your second chin off."

Baz shrugged. "I tried," he said, taking a few steps back

66

Luke James

from the water.

The fin reappeared on the other side of the soldier. It seemed to just float there, biding its time. The soldier raised his fists above the surface, as if ready to box the shark to death.

Then, as quick as a papercut, the fin lurched towards him. Rows of razor-like teeth leapt from the water, taking a chunk out of his torso.

The soldier cried out and fell backwards into the water. His head vanished beneath the surface while his arms still thrashed around in plain sight.

The splashes turned red. After a few seconds, they died down, leaving only ripples.

The scene was peaceful again.

"Now I see why the ducks didn't come back," Baz said.

They heard calls from the other side of the park as more soldiers came towards them. They had guns in their hands and they looked angry.

Luke James

CHAPTER NINE

On their knees, rifles pointed at their heads, Norman, Baz and the girl watched the soldiers with bemusement as they threw stick after stick of dynamite into the pond, trying to blow up the shark. Each time they failed. The fin kept reappearing in a different area of the pond. In the end, one clever grunt went to his tank and came back with a harpoon gun.

It was a group effort to attach the dynamite to the harpoon, and then a fifteen minute argument over who was the best shot. In the end Major Pierce pulled rank and took it himself. The senior officer must have had a lot of confidence in his own ability; failing to make the shot would result in humiliation. Norman knew soldiers would never explicitly belittle someone of senior rank, but they would all have seen it. It would turn the Major's ego into an even less predictable beast.

He raised the harpoon gun to his face and pointed it at the circling fin. One of the grunts lit the fuse. It was hard to tell how long he had before the fuse would run out, but with it burning just a few inches from his face, he must have felt the pressure. If he did, he did well to hide it.

The wick burned quickly, forcing him to take the shot. It was a perfect strike, piercing the centre of the fin. The soldiers gasped, but saved their cheers for after the blast. The creature thrashed, but its time had run out. The explosion came.

A cocktail of pond water and shark guts rained over

the surrounding area and everyone in it. The soldiers, as well as Norman, Baz and the girl, were covered in red goo.

Norman cringed at the overpowering stench of fish. A set of dogtags landed a few feet from him, clearly belonging to the soldier who had been eaten by the shark.

"Yuck," Baz muttered.

One of the soldiers started laughing, and then the others joined in. Once again they raised their guns in celebration.

"Embrace the smell of victory, boys!" Major Pierce commanded, clearly buoyed after making the shot.

Norman found it amazing how excited they were about blowing up a fish. Not all soldiers were such tossers, he assured himself. There were, of course, very nice and noble ones in the real world. But Fury had clearly put these ones into the model world to torment him, so it made sense that they represented the most despicable concept of a soldier.

"What we gonna do 'bout these three?" asked the grunt pointing a gun at Norman's head.

Through squinted eyes, Fury could see Norman's glow inside the town hall. She could still feel his presence too, as if he was in the room with her. That gave her comfort – she hadn't killed him.

The old sadistic instincts had come back, reminding her of just how much she'd changed since being with Norman – on the timescale of an immortal, she'd only been with him for a sliver.

Having had a long break from using it, she'd got used to the magic, in particular how it impacted on the miniature world. Norman had crafted the creative essence when he built it – she'd used those seeds to nurture it to life. But now he was trapped inside, and the essence was solely

Luke James

hers to tinker with. Each change she made would unravel in the spirit she intended. It would play out its course and consequences, and keep going, until she made another change. She could pick up a miniature person and move them to the other side of the world, and they would carry on as though they had always been there. It was the same with the buildings, and the new elements she added each time.

She delved into the box at her feet. It was full of toys, some more recent ones from Malice's childhood, and some older ones from Norman's. A melancholy swept over her as, with each reach and rummage, she uncovered more artefacts from his youth – evidence of a more innocent time, before she'd met him, before he'd thawed her heart where no hellfire could. That was one of the things that had turned her demon world upside down in the first place: his innocence, his earnestness, his child-like candour. It went against everything she'd been raised to believe about humans.

She had come to the jarring realisation that her preconceptions about humanity had been solely based on the narrow experience offered to her by the vulgar dregs that tumbled into her dimension. Souls deemed corrupt enough to be diverted for damnation weren't the best ambassadors for the depth and diversity of the race as a whole.

This revelation had first come to her when a truly lost soul had been misdirected into her pit, or rather her dimension - an administrative "cock-up" some might call it. It was quickly corrected, but the experience had already left its mark on Fury the moment she encountered the unfortunate individual. It was what started everything – what led her to Earth, to Norman.

Model Railway Apocalypse

Her conceptions had been shattered once again when she walked in on Norman and that tart, flipping her world upside down. Not in a million years – and she might just live that long – would she have predicted he would betray her like that. Now her grasp on reality was twisted and out of her control. She no longer trusted the real world – but she could shape this miniature one.

Her mother had been so disappointed by her past choices, but she'd be so proud of her now. And where was the bitch? She could use her right now, while her resolve was weakened. Even though they hadn't been on good terms recently, Ferocity had been a staggering force in her life – a creature of strength and conviction – and even though she didn't agree with everything her mother said, Fury would always listen.

The only other person she ever really listened to was Norman. She missed his wisdom and perceptiveness. It was funny to her that some creatures live forever with rigid, one-dimensional convictions, while others exist only for a few blinks of sunlight, but would somehow manage to form profound insights. Mortals were funnier too – having no choice but to laugh at their own transience. "You live, you have therapy, then you die," Norman used to say. Fury couldn't help but smile as she reflected on some of his cruder jokes.

Had she really seen what she thought she'd seen? Had she maybe reacted too quickly?

She pulled a robot and some model dinosaurs out of the box.

Luke James

CHAPTER TEN

Getting to a phone wasn't going well. Norman found himself tied to a chair in the town hall, guarded by a lone soldier with a gun. Also tied to chairs were Baz and the girl they'd helped. They were still covered in shark guts and, after he'd bombarded the soldiers with a boundless torrent of nauseatingly lewd verbal abuse, Norman's mouth had been taped shut, for fear of offending someone's grandma. The flowers were still tucked into the large pocket of his gown – although they were becoming slightly mangled.

Clearly over his mourning for the fallen giantess, Baz was making small talk with the girl.

"Do you have a name or can I just call you 'Mine'?"

She giggled.

"It's Julie."

"Lovely to meet you, Julie. Can I call you 'Jewel'?"

She giggled some more.

"Okay."

Norman let out a groan which, with the tape over his mouth, consisted only of vowels.

"Don't worry about him," Baz said. "He's just sulky 'cause his wife's pissed with him."

Julie smiled.

The soldier was sitting in the corner, leaning against the wall with his gun on the floor. He was holding the fallen soldier's dogtags and saying a prayer. What a cliché, Norman thought. Not only were these soldiers abusive

73

Model Railway Apocalypse

egomaniacs, but they thought they were serving God.

"Did it hurt when you fell from heaven?" Baz asked Julie.

She laughed out loud. Norman vomited. With the tape over his mouth, he had to swallow it again.

"Are you sure he's okay?" Julie asked.

"Yeah, he's just not feeling very well. I'm not either, but my doctor says I'm just missing vitamin U." Baz's stupid grin belonged on a baby who'd just discovered bubbles.

Norman couldn't take it anymore. This was becoming worse than any torture Fury could visit on him. He had to do something so he cried out as if he was in pain.

"Mmmm mmmh mmh mmmmmph," was all that could be heard under the tape.

The soldier stood up.

"What the fuck's the matter with you?"

What was it with these soldiers and the f-word?

"Mmm mmmmh mmmmph."

The soldier walked over to him. "What's that you're saying?"

"Norman, are you okay?" Baz asked. The soldier smacked Baz around the head.

"Shut up!"

"Mmmmph!"

The soldier ripped the tape from Norman's mouth, leaving his lips stinging.

"Speak!" he demanded.

"I said," Norman began, pausing to glance at Baz and Julie, who were watching eagerly. He licked the dryness from his lips, then looked the soldier directly in the eye.

"Does my dick taste right to you?"

"What the fuck did you say to me?" the soldier moved his face right up close to Norman's. Norman head-butted him as hard as he could. The grunt fell to the floor unconscious.

74

Luke James

Baz and Julie glared at him, open-mouthed.

"Now that's a pick-up line."

"Holy shit, buddy!!"

"Shut up, big man, and get us untied before another guard comes." Norman's head pounded and his eyesight was fuzzy. He'd never nutted anyone before and the soldier's head was harder than he'd expected.

"Me?"

"What's the point in being built like a wrestler if you can't wrestle your way out of some rope?"

At that Baz seemed to rediscover the same determination and die-hard heroism he'd demonstrated in tackling the giantess. He writhed and wrestled against the rope. It wouldn't budge. He wriggled and rocked and caused the chair to bounce up and down while he made violent thrusting movements.

It was a little disturbing to watch - much like when he slid out from the dead giant woman's cleavage. If the outcome wasn't so vital to his getting free, Norman would have turned away.

Eventually it was the chair and not the rope that broke. He landed on his backside with a thump, and grumbled in pain. But he was free; the rope was loose.

"That's great," Norman said. "Now untie us."

Baz leapt to his feet and untied Julie first, then Norman. With his head still pounding Norman stood up. A heavy black cloud fell over his vision and he tried to fight it back, closing his eyes for a moment and steadying his footing. But it wasn't enough.

Oblivion latched onto him like a parasite, and he fell to the floor.

Luke James

CHAPTER ELEVEN

Night moved through her strange blue body while the radio hummed its melancholic song. Her bare legs glowed in the flickering of the muted television as she sat on the sofa, an immortal Goddess on a throne. He leant against the doorframe, wearing only his boxer-shorts and the camera hanging around his neck, wondering how best to savour the moment: a photograph or a memory? Had anyone ever photographed a demon before?

First she'd told him what she was, over dinner in the local Italian. He didn't have much trouble believing her; everything about her already seemed otherworldly to him, from the night they met - the suddenness of it, the strangeness – to right now, where he still lingered under her unending spell. As he came to know her, the strangeness of how it happened faded away. It didn't matter. Neither did whether or not he believed her now.

When they'd got home from dinner, she'd shown him her true form. How had she managed to keep it hidden all this time? After all, they'd spent so much of their time naked. But now here she was, naked-naked. Why had she kept it hidden from him? He supposed it was to avoid frightening him. As she stood there, with eyes that glowed like the evening sun and a willowy tail that snaked in the air like wildfire, there was nothing much scary about her to him - except for the depth of her beauty.

She wasn't beyond recognition. The heat in her eyes, the shape of her smile, and the way she moved were all

Model Railway Apocalypse

still Fury – a name he finally believed was her own, and not just some punky nickname. She still kissed and made love like the woman he'd come to know, and that's exactly what they did. Only this time, she seemed more confident, more in control, more liberal with her powerful form.

"I'm starting to get worried about him. Do you think he's okay?" The soft voice seemed to travel down a tunnel before it reached Norman's ears. His head felt six feet under ground and upside down. The smoky smell of coal assaulted his nostrils. "He's been out a long time."

"He's just taking some time out." The second voice was a little more familiar. "Let's just sit tight until he comes around."

Gunfire rapped in the distance. A thudding came and went like a passing giant.

"I'm not sure we're safe here."

There were mechanical noises, like concrete crushed under metal.

"I don't think we're safe anywhere. At least the soldiers don't know we're here."

An explosion. Agonised screaming.

"Look, he's stirring."

A hand fell on Norman's shoulder, another on his head. There was heavy breathing. He opened his eyes. It was blurry at first, and dark. The blurriness faded but the darkness remained as his eyes worked to focus on the large man and the woman leaning over him.

"There you are, buddy!" Baz chirped. The baby-faced grin was a welcome sight, even if it was accompanied by the sound of a rocket tearing through the skies outside and striking some large object.

Norman hadn't forgotten the plan: get to a phone so he

78

Luke James

could try calling Fury.

"Phone," he mumbled through lips that didn't seem to want to move.

"Phone?" Julie repeated.

"Phone...home..."

"He wants to phone home," Baz said. "Don't worry buddy, we'll get you to a phone as soon as the little apocalypse outside has died down."

"Apocalypse?"

Baz chuckled, not in a reassuring way. "You've missed a few things. We'll catch you up."

Norman sat upright.

"Take your time," Julie said. "You've probably got a concussion."

"Explains why the ground is moving," Norman assured himself.

"No, actually, it really is moving," Baz said. "But it's probably twice as bad for you."

They seemed to be inside a small building, like a garden shed or an outhouse, with the lights switched off.

"Where are we?"

"We're just hiding out in a coal shed for a while," Baz said. There were shrieking and screeching noises outside, like giant birds of prey were swooping through the town.

"Why?"

The door was slightly ajar, but Baz opened it a little more so Norman could see out. It was hard to make out anything clearly – it was night time and there was a lot of smoke and fog – but he could see shadowy figures running about in the darkness – soldiers or civilians, he assumed. There were fires scattered around the scene. He saw someone moving just a few meters away, running quickly and then pausing, darting and pausing again. He couldn't

79

Model Railway Apocalypse

make out any detail but when they passed in front of a fire he saw the silhouette – this was no human. It had a tail, a long neck with a reptilian head and crooked arms with sharp, razor-like claws.

The realisation dawned: Fury had discovered his old dinosaur models. He had quite the collection from his childhood, which meant there wouldn't just be one monster. There would be an entire hoard of different species.

He could see now what the gunfire was all about; the soldiers were at war with the dinosaurs.

"Right," Norman said. "Now I see why we're hiding in the coal shed."

Light from the flames crept through the gap in the door, illuminating Baz and Julie. Baz was dressed in a soldier's uniform. When had he got changed? Who had he taken it from? Both of their faces and their clothes were blackened with coal. Pretty good camouflage in the darkness, Norman thought. The smell might also help conceal them from the dinosaurs.

"How did we get here?"

"Well..." Baz paused, as if trying to remember. "You knocked out the guard and ended up knocking yourself out too. But it gave us time to get free, get his gun and escape the town hall."

"You carried me?"

"Well, my back's still a bit put out from being crushed in that giant woman's cleavage, and I was carrying the gun, so Jewel here did most of the heavy lifting."

The little woman shrugged and smiled as though it was nothing.

"As we were leaving the town hall the soldiers were having a barbeque party with pieces of dead shark. There

Luke James

was no way they'd just let us walk. So I thought it would be a good idea if I went back and switched clothes with the soldier you knocked out, and then pretend I was escorting you as prisoners. Making Julie carry you would make me appear just as badass as the rest of them."

"Did it work?"

"Not for a second. They recognised me immediately. But then the dinos turn up and everything went to hell anyway. The soldiers were distracted and Jewel and I snuck away. Fortunately the dinos seemed more interested in the soldiers, who were making a riot and going for their guns. We made it to the coal shed and we've been here for the last two hours."

"Thanks for not leaving me behind."

"Never!"

Norman checked his pockets and panicked.

"Did you remember my flowers?"

"Oh, yeah!" Baz rummaged around in the crack between his butt cheeks and pulled out the hyacinths, which were beyond mangled, but still retained some of their purple petals. He presented them to Norman proudly.

"Thanks," Norman said, with a mix of gratitude and unease. He tucked them back in to the pocket of his gown, determined to give them to Fury at the first opportunity. If he could get to a phone, and did happen to get through to her and explain himself, all the chaos – the dinosaurs and the soldiers and all the madness – would end.

"I need to go out there," he said. "I need to get to a phone." Norman knew for a fact there were no mobile phones in this town. This had been based on his ideal place to live after all, and he was not a fan of mobiles – although he regretted that now.

"Buddy, your wife can wait. She won't want you dead."

Model Railway Apocalypse

Norman shook his head.

"You don't understand. If I can get to a phone, I might be able to end the reign of chaos in Furydale. Everything that's been happening here is because of me."

"No. I'm not having you blame yourself for a few strokes of bad luck."

"That's very touching. I can't explain, but I think I can end it. Now where's the nearest phone?"

"You got God's number or somethin'?" Baz asked.

"'Or something'. Where is it?"

"On the platform, I think," Julie said. "We're about three-hundred feet from the station."

"Great. Stay here. I'm going to scope it out. See if there's a clear path."

Baz tried to offer Norman his gun, but he refused. There was only one of him and two of them. They agreed Baz and Julie would use it to cover him while he did his recon of the nearby area. Norman covered himself in coal, hoping it'd camouflage him from the nightmares outside. They were a little way from the town. The station was further still.

"Buddy?" Baz whispered to Norman as he was about to step outside.

"Yeah?"

"I shot a raptor in the head...right between the eyes. It was pretty intense."

"That's brilliant," Norman said, smiling and patting him on the back. "That'll make a much better chat-up line."

The larger man grinned, and Norman stepped out into the night.

Luke James

CHAPTER TWELVE

The air was smoky and humid, but it still felt fresher than inside the coal shed. As he breathed, Norman wondered whether the air he inhaled was the same as that in the spare room where he'd built his model railway – where his wife must be now, deliberately pulling it apart. Did they breathe the same air? These were deep questions he didn't have time to entertain.

Still, he couldn't shake the idea that somewhere above him the love of his life lingered in the skies, toying with his world. He imagined her in her full sexy demon glory. Where had that passion been in recent years?

He set his questions to one side, slowly and stealthily traversing the hazardous terrain towards the train station, keeping his eye out for ferocious dinosaurs or psychotic soldiers.

There was a stegosaurus corpse lying part way to the station. Norman ducked down behind its muscular leg, which made for a good place to pause and evaluate progress. He scanned the chaotic horizon, stopping for a double-take at the largest object, the size of a grand hotel, rolling smoothly through the town, mounting and flattening cars as though they were plastic bottles. It was still some distance away, but that didn't stop Norman recognising his old toy robot, Killbot, with its shiny grey armour and bulky, undiscriminating caterpillar-tracks. It had laser guns attached to the sides of its retro box-shaped head, which it was putting to full use, disintegrating

83

Model Railway Apocalypse

anything that moved. It approached the Town Hall.

Norman watched in awe as it crushed the building beneath its giant treads. The building fell apart as if it was made of cardboard.

He knew he had to move quickly. He was almost at the station.

He jumped out from behind the deceased dinosaur and ran through the mist and fog. Occasionally he ran by a fallen soldier or civilian. More often than not they had limbs missing. Most seemed to be dead, but some quietly groaned. Trying not to look too closely, Norman kept running.

Finally he ran up the stairs and through the station building onto the platform. There was The Phoenix - the large steam locomotive - stopped in the station, with half a dozen carriages. It didn't look as though it was going anywhere anytime soon. There was a public payphone a little way up the platform.

He cursed as he realised he didn't have any money. It had been lost along with the rest of his luggage inside The Shaggy Dog.

"No change, dude?" asked a deep, booming voice. It made him jump, and echoed around the station.

Norman glanced about, trying to identify the source.

"Over here, by the platform."

He still couldn't tell where it came from. It was hard to tell in the dark and smoky night, but there didn't seem to be anyone else on the platform. With the locomotive stopped at the station, he couldn't see to the opposite platform to work out if the voice came from there.

"Down here. On the tracks."

He walked along the platform and noticed a body lying between the rails a few meters in front of the train. It was

Luke James

a man, though he was clearly dead - his head was twisted the wrong way - so couldn't be the one talking to him.

"No dude, look up!"

Norman did and saw the huge, metallic face, watching him with a grubby grin that struck terror into his heart. The Phoenix was alive, and talking to him.

"There you go," it said. "No change, huh?"

Norman stood frozen on the platform. The giant mechanical face stared at him, eyes wide. Norman managed to shake his head, his mouth hanging wide open.

"Not to worry, dude," the locomotive said. "I know where you can get some."

Norman swallowed.

"See this poor dude down here?" the Phoenix went on.

Norman nodded, turning his gaze to the body lying on the tracks.

"I'm pretty sure he's got a wallet in his pocket."

"You want me to take the dead guy's wallet?" Norman was finally able to speak.

"Sure man, he doesn't need it."

Even after everything, this seemed dark, especially coming from something that resembled a popular children's television character.

Norman glanced up and down the platform.

"Don't beat yourself up. You need to make a call, right? Pretty badly by the look of it."

Norman peered again over the edge of the platform.

"What happened to him?"

"Poor little dude had a heart attack and fell off the platform. That's all, man. Game over."

"No one helped him?"

"Not sure if you've noticed, but things have taken a crazy turn in this town lately. Who's gonna stop and help some

Model Railway Apocalypse

guy having a heart attack? There are prehistoric beasts running wild, for Heaven's sake! Not to mention the terminator rampaging through town."

Norman contemplated his situation: this guy was dead - if he did have any change, he wouldn't be using it. Norman would. With it he could end all of this.

"Go on, dude. I won't tell."

Norman pulled his gown tightly around himself, and slid off the platform onto the track. He ran his hands over the guy's pocket, feeling a wallet-shaped bulge inside.

Before he could reach in and pull it out, the locomotive expelled a large plume of smoke and lurched towards him.

"Jesus!" Norman shouted, leaping back on to the platform only inches shy of the two-hundred ton monster. He rolled away from the edge taking sharp, panicked breaths.

"What the hell?" he gasped at the locomotive.

"What is it, dude?"

"You were about to mow me down!"

"Huh?"

"You tried to kill me!"

"Woah, man. I did no such thing." It sounded genuinely hurt. "Why would I do that?"

"Because you're a sadistic psychopath!"

"Not me, man – you've got the wrong guy."

Norman looked again over the edge of the platform at the body, which now lay barely two feet in front of the train. He could see the corner of the guy's wallet poking out of his pocket.

"I promise, dude. I'm not trying to kill you," the locomotive said. "Go on. Take the guy's wallet. He doesn't need it."

Norman wasn't taking any chances. He lay flat on his front and leaned over the edge, reaching down towards

Luke James

the dead man. His fingertips brushed the pocket. Just a little stretch and he'd be able to grab it. He wiggled on his hips, shuffling closer, awkwardly extending his reach.

Gears churned and scraped as the brutish engine dashed forwards again.

Norman flinched, barely tucking his arms back beneath him in time.

"Damnit!"

"What?" the train pleaded. "Come on, just once more. I promise I won't move."

Norman shook his head, walking away. Taking this dead man's wallet was no longer worth it. He'd have to rethink.

"Ah, man. You're no fun," the locomotive grumbled as Norman walked down the platform. "I'll see you later, dude," the train taunted.

Luke James

CHAPTER THIRTEEN

As Norman made his way back to the coal shed where Baz and Julie were hiding, the messy skyline caught his eye. Killbot was making his way through the buildings, systematically bulldozing them to the ground while screams still echoed around the town. In the model world, they had nowhere to run, no release but death – unless he could get to a phone and end this. At the rate the giant robot was going, the chances of there being a building left containing a working phone were quickly shrinking. Norman would have to move fast.

He'd almost reached the coal shed when he heard the padding of large feet getting louder. Coming towards him through the mists was the hulking frame of a triceratops. The prehistoric animal charged with all three horns pointed at him.

Norman glanced at the shed, wondering if he could make a run for it. But the tiny structure was only made of wood, and if Baz and Julie were still inside, they'd surely be crushed if the beast chased him.

He considered sprinting in another direction, trying to outrun the dinosaur. That didn't look likely either; it was moving too fast.

All he could do was dodge it by jumping out of the way at the last minute. He readied himself to spring to one side, hoping the creature's agility didn't match its straight line speed.

How long should he wait? He could see its eyes now,

Model Railway Apocalypse

yellow and angry. Only a few meters away, it showed no sign of slowing.

Norman bent his knees.

Just when he was about to jump, the beast exploded. Norman closed his eyes, instinctively protecting them from the spray of dinosaur guts splattering on his face and gown.

"Woohoo!" a mad voice cried out.

A figure strutted towards him, heavily armed with two rifles and two pistols. It didn't take Norman long to recognise the silver-haired, military man. Major Pierce had a manic grimace on his face as he came through the smoky air. His smile quickly dropped as soon as he saw Norman.

"Wait a second," he said, stopping just a few feet away. "I saved you?"

Norman nodded.

"Ah, damn. That was my last grenade." He frowned in frustration. "Never mind," he said, his sick smile returning. "I'll just have to shoot you instead."

Norman tilted his head, wondering if perhaps he'd misheard the Major's comment. But the military man raised his rifles, pointing them both at him.

"Why?" he protested.

"You're the tit who lampooned me in front of my men."

"Yeah, but you're going to shoot me with both guns?"

"Well...yeah."

"Why?"

"Because I want to kill you."

"Couldn't you kill me with just one? Why do you have to use both guns at once?"

"Because it's more fun for me."

The soldier's stupidity was staggering. Norman

Luke James

wondered whether Baz was watching from the coal shed. Wasn't the big man supposed to be covering his back?

"Seems like a tragic waste of ammo," Norman said, stalling for time. "What with all the dinosaurs and that giant robot. Don't you think you should save some?"

"All the dinosaurs are dead. I'll be damned if I'm going anywhere near that robot. Look, just shut the fuck up while I kill you."

"I'm just wondering about the wisdom of using two guns on a single, unarmed civilian."

"Consider yourself lucky I can't hold more than two at once."

Norman was determined he wasn't going to go out like this - killed by one of his toy soldiers inside the model railway he built himself.

Come on Baz, he thought. Where are you?

"Are you sure?" Norman continued.

"What?"

"Are you sure you can't hold more than two at a time?"

"Don't get cute." The Major eased his fingers on the triggers.

"Have you tried?" Norman asked.

The Major seemed to ponder this for a while, looking down at the rifles in his hands and the pistols tucked into his hips. Could he actually do it?

"Go on, give it a go."

He lowered one of the rifles, and stretched his trigger finger towards one of the pistols. Awkwardly, he struggled to grip the smaller gun while maintaining his grip on the rifle. He cursed to himself, becoming increasingly irate.

A huge explosion echoed across the town.

Both men looked up to see the top had blown off the highest peak. Magma flew into the sky as if from a shaken-

Model Railway Apocalypse

up champagne bottle. Norman and Major Pierce ducked down as the burning ooze rained down around them. Rivers of it ran down the side of the hills, towards the town.

"Fuck it," the Major said, lifting his rifle again. He pointed it at Norman and pulled the trigger.

Several shots rang out. The Major dropped to the floor next to the dead dinosaur.

"That's for the giant woman," Baz said coolly. Through the falling skies, he and Julie came walking from the coal shed, both with ruffled hair.

"Sorry for the delay, Norman. We were a little distracted."

"Better late than never, I suppose."

"How did the phone call go?" Julie asked.

"It didn't. It was a payphone. I didn't have any change."

"Oh no, I'm sorry." Baz checked his pockets. "I don't have any either."

"Nevermind," Norman said. "But it looks as if heading back into town is our only option. There should be a land line there somewhere."

They eyed the volcanic eruption and the giant robot. Both still rolled along threatening to destroy everything in their path.

"Reckon we can make it?" Baz asked.

"We have to."

"We'd better be quick then or there won't be a town left."

92

Luke James

CHAPTER FOURTEEN

The town was barely recognisable, not just as the town he had built and named after his wife, but as a town at all. Most of the buildings looked as if they'd been ripped open from the corners, like Christmas presents unwrapped and strewn about by a spoilt child. Quiet fires burned inside the structures, while fumes burned inside Norman's lungs; the air was thick with ash. He and his companions covered their mouths as they crept into town, darting between the husks of cars to keep out of the eye-line of the giant robot.

Through the thick toxic air, it was hard to tell if there were any survivors. Bodies of soldiers and civilians peppered the streets. The cars had been reshaped into strange sculptures, like mutant machines. The tarmac was cracked and crumbled like the Devil's golf-course, crushed under the giant caterpillar tracks of Killbot. The metal behemoth no longer fired lasers. Perhaps it had finally extinguished all life in the town, but it still patrolled the streets, seeming oblivious to the approaching lava which flowed down from the peak.

Camouflaged by the coal-dust and ash, Norman, Baz and Julie ducked behind a wall, which used to be the side of the general store, but was now free-standing – for the time being. They were careful not to lean on it too heavily or their cover would be blown and the robot would be alerted to their presence – and have a clear shot.

"So which building looks as if it might still have a working phone?" Baz whispered, peering through the

Model Railway Apocalypse

hole in the wall where a window used to be.

"I'm not sure. Everything this end is just heaps of rubble," Norman said.

"That row of houses," Julie pointed down the street. "One of them must have a working phone."

"But that's where the robot is," Baz warned.

"Doesn't look like much hope this end," Julie said.

Behind them the building that used to house the swimming pool had been decimated, leaving the sorry-looking puddle exposed. Bodies floated on the surface. Across the street a dead tyrannosaur slumped in the ruins of the bookshop.

"She's right," Norman said. "We've got to try that row of houses."

"But the lava will hit that end of the town any minute. It's too dangerous," Baz warned.

"I don't see much choice."

"What about the robot?"

This wasn't going to be easy. Baz and Julie had shown such loyalty in just a short amount of time. To ask the pair for more seemed like taking advantage. But Norman needed them.

"You don't have to do this. This is my mission."

Baz shook his head. "But this is our problem too. Look around. Where else are we gonna go?"

"I'm not even sure where I came from," Julie said. "I was just here."

"Same here. As far as I'm concerned I come from the pub," Baz added. "But that can't be right."

"Nothing's quite right here." They both shook their heads ruefully.

"We're with you, buddy," Baz said, grinning. "Let's get you to a phone!"

94

Luke James

Norman nodded. He supposed they were right. They were here because of him. Their well-being depended on him getting to a phone and getting through to Fury – if that would even work. And his getting to a phone depended on their help.

"How about this: you two distract the big, scary robot – try and lure him this way if you can – and I'll pick my way around the back streets towards those terraced houses, hopefully before the lava hits."

"It's a plan!"

"As soon as you've got its attention, you run for cover. Got it?"

They nodded.

Luke James

CHAPTER FIFTEEN

"Why do we torture humans?" the young demoness asked as she walked along the rocky walkway. Her mother held her hand, protecting her from the sheer drop on either side.

"Because, my dear Fury, evil must be punished," Ferocity replied. Although her horns were still just two little lumps on her head, yet to break the skin, the fledgling demoness had to learn about reality – about her people's duty. Sooner or later, a visit to the pits was a rite of passage undertaken by all demons. Bring-your-daughter-to-work day was the perfect opportunity.

"What makes them evil?"

"They do bad things."

"Like what?"

"Many humans deliberately hurt or betray others. They're dishonourable and deceitful and like to cause pain. They steal and commit violence and rape and murder. They choose frivolous lifestyles focused only on themselves, watching reality television and caking themselves in fake tan while others suffer. Some drive BMWs and don't even indicate before changing lanes. These are corrupt, capricious individuals who make bad choices and the Great Lord doesn't want them ruining his Holy Houseparty. So they come here instead."

"Are all humans evil?" the young demoness asked, peering over the edge at the garden of pits, which stretched out to the horizon either side of them.

Model Railway Apocalypse

"Apparently not. Some are supposedly good. Good enough, at least, to make it to the Sacred Shindig."

"And the evil ones come here?" The girl's amber eyes moved from one grimy pit to another, each containing a cursed human, and the demon custodian assigned to torture them. Wardens patrolled the perimeters of the pits. Her chest thumped with excitement that one day this would be her office. Groans and whimpers filled the air, occasionally pierced by a scream or a howl.

"That's right, my dear."

"Abomina said not all humans stay here forever. Is that true?"

"Yes. In fact most leave, eventually. When a custodian believes the human has paid their penance, they will recommend they be moved on. They will go before The Judge who has the final say."

"Uncle Slander?" the young demon asked, excited.

"That's right. Your uncle will determine if they are ready to leave."

"How does he decide?"

"Uncle Slander is a wise demon."

"What happens to them when they leave?"

"There are a few possible options. Some of them, the lucky ones, get an invitation to Heaven after all. Others go to another place, a bit like the Blessed Bash, except without the angels and the free booze. Some of them are sent back to Earth to live as animals."

"What about the ones who don't leave?"

"They are returned to the pit, given a new custodian, until their penance is served."

"What if it is never served?"

The mother smiled. "The best custodians get it right the first time."

Luke James

"Will I be a custodian one day?"
"You can be whatever you like, my dear Fury."

Luke James

CHAPTER SIXTEEN

Slowly and vigilantly, Killbot rolled down the street with the terraced houses, away from where Baz and Julie were hiding behind the free-standing wall. They watched Norman carefully, as he ducked behind the metal skeletons of cars and the piles of rubble, making steady progress without giving himself away. But now he'd reached a crossroads, and getting to the other side safely would be difficult. It was time to cause a distraction.

"Are you ready?" Baz asked Julie.

"I was ready five minutes ago."

"As soon as we do this, we'll need to run."

"I hope you can keep up." She smiled and kissed his cheek. "Let's do it."

Baz raised the rifle into the air and pulled the trigger. The weapon clicked, but didn't fire. He pulled the trigger again. Still nothing.

"Is the safety on?" Julie asked.

"I don't think it has one," he said, examining the gun.

"Let's have a look." She took the weapon and ejected the magazine. She shook it in her hands. "Empty."

Baz was impressed by her apparent expertise in firearms.

"Shit. Look, Norman's about to cross," he said.

"We need another distraction."

Baz sighed and leant against the wall, hanging his head.

The whole wall swayed. He jerked away quickly, in case it came crashing down.

101

Model Railway Apocalypse

"Wait," Julie said. She put all of her weight against the large brick surface and gritted her teeth. "Help me!"

The large man did as he was told. Together they pushed the wall away from them. It didn't take much force for it to collapse, causing a loud crash as it joined the pile of rubble behind.

Baz stood for a moment, mouth-gaping at the destruction. Julie tugged at his sleeve, pulling him from his reverie.

"Come on!"

A flurry of bright red laser-fire struck the pile of rubble where the wall had fallen. Baz and Julie fled into the night.

First he heard the crash, then the laser-fire, then the heavy grind of caterpillar tracks as the mechanical monster accelerated, surprisingly fast, towards Baz and Julie. Harrowing in its display of aggression, it shot poisoned light from both sides of its head.

Norman hoped his friends would be quick enough to escape. He had to fight the temptation not to go back to make sure they were okay. That would be counter-productive. Maybe they needed him, but what they really needed was for him to carry out the plan, and for it to work. He knew he was taking a gamble with this phone idea, but he didn't have any other ideas. If it didn't work, he'd probably have to go back to sitting around hoping Fury would have a change of heart.

This had to work.

He examined the scene in front of him: a crumbling street lined with half-demolished houses, grubby from falling ash, backlit by the warm glow of lava oozing down from the hills. On one side of the street, the frontages of

Luke James

the terraced houses had been ripped away by Killbot's broad caterpillar tracks, allowing an X-ray view into the once-cosy abodes. On the other side, the houses remained largely intact. He figured there was every chance of finding a phone on either side, but maybe those with less damage were more likely to have a working line.

The distant ping of laser-fire told him the robot was well and truly distracted. He left his hiding place and ran towards the row of houses. From the outside they looked abandoned.

Despite the apparent lack of immediate danger, Norman still found himself crouching low as he moved, determined not to draw attention to himself.

He approached the first house in the street and walked up the short path to the red front door. He pushed lightly on the off-chance it would open, but it wouldn't budge. There was no way to open it without a key.

He glanced at the windows at the front of the house to see if any were open or broken. Amazingly, the glass was all still intact and sealed shut. Breaking in would mean smashing a window; the noise would likely draw the robot back in his direction. He moved on to the next house.

It was the mirror image of the first. This one had a blue door, which also wouldn't budge.

Noxious fumes filled his nostrils. The lava had reached the end of the street. Houses were starting to crumble from the bottom up. He couldn't afford to waste time grappling with doors that didn't open.

He took a step back and scanned the row of houses. A window was part-way open on the ground floor only two doors away. He darted across the tiny front gardens. The pane was propped open on a latch, hinged on its side. Climbing in would be easy. Nevertheless, he erred

Model Railway Apocalypse

on the side of caution, avoiding making any noises as he gently lifted the latch, eased the window open wider and slipped inside.

The living room was modestly-sized, decorated with pale yellow wallpaper. A small, brown sofa and an armchair faced a fireplace. It reminded Norman of his grandparents' house from when he was a child – very little colour, immaculately clean; it wasn't the kind of place a young grandson looked forward to visiting.

There was no sign of a phone. His grandparents had kept their phone in the hall by the stairs. Maybe that's where he'd find one in this house.

The hallway was small with green carpet and landscape paintings which hung crooked on the wall. Still no sign of a phone. Norman noticed a door closed at the end of the hallway. Must be the kitchen he thought. Some people keep their phones in their kitchen.

When he opened the door, his suspicions were confirmed: it was the kitchen. What he didn't expect to see however, was a gleaming row of needle like teeth as a raptor grimaced at him. Its hulking frame turned slowly towards him. Its large yellow eyes studied him. It seemed to smile at Norman, as if thinking: I bet you taste good.

With a skull-piercing scream, the raptor launched at him. He ducked down; it was becoming his natural reaction to The reptile tumbled forwards over him, landing awkwardly in the hallway. Norman ran into the cramped kitchen and scanned the surfaces for something to use to defend himself. A knife would be ideal, but there weren't any lying around.

The raptor was back on its feet. It ran at him. Norman flipped the small kitchen table towards it, causing it to stumble forwards awkwardly.

He opened the drawer closest to him. Still no knives. He grabbed the first thing he could, which happened to be a wooden spoon. The raptor came at him again.

Norman struck it in the eye with the wooden spoon.

Unsurprisingly the ferocious reptile only flinched a little. Its yellow eye quickly recovered and refocused on its prey.

It snapped its jaws at him. Norman side-stepped, feeling its breath on his ear as it barely missed him. It snapped again and again while Norman ducked and dodged, opening more drawers in search of a decent weapon. His hands frantically felt for something useable. They found a spatula, then a whisk.

As he frantically fumbled through the drawers, the raptor caught him off-guard, sinking its teeth into his shoulder. Norman screamed as it pierced his flesh and tugged, trying to tear off his arm. Finally his free arm found a saucepan and smacked the raptor around the head as hard as he could. It seemed momentarily stunned, letting go of his shoulder. A second strike and it stumbled, trying to remain upright.

Norman heard his own heart beat thumping in his chest. Blood poured from his shoulder and he was losing feeling in his arm.

The creature seemed to struggle to stay conscious. A final firm strike knocked it to the floor. Its eyes fell shut.

Without wasting time, Norman scanned the room for a phone. He noticed a warm glow dancing through the kitchen window, as though the ground was on fire.

He leaned over the sink to look outside. The lava had made it to the next house. He could hear it whispering as

Model Railway Apocalypse

it burned away at the foundations.

There was no sign of a phone in here. There was only one more place to check. Norman huffed when he saw a sharp bread knife lying in the kitchen sink. He thought about using it to finish the raptor off, but carving its head off it while it slept seemed a little heartless. He tucked the blade in the pocket of his gown, alongside what was left of the hyacinths.

He stepped quietly over the drooling monster to exit the kitchen. As he approached the door, he felt a tugging on his gown, as though he'd got it caught on a drawer handle. Without turning around, he gave it a gentle pull. But it didn't work. He looked over his shoulder and saw the yellow eyes were open. Large smiling jaws clasped the fabric of his robe.

The raptor leapt to its feet, shaking its head groggily. Its nap was clearly over. Norman backed away into the hallway, tearing his robe. He moved as slowly as possible, as though it would deter the monster from attacking.

It spat out the shred of fabric and leant forwards, ready to charge. Norman slipped the breadknife out of his pocket and raised it to defend himself. The creature exhaled, two misty puffs flaring from each nostril.

It let out a screeching battle cry and ran at him.

Norman leant forward and pulled the kitchen door closed with his good arm. He heard a thump as the raptor struck the other side.

The door didn't budge. Good solid oak, Norman thought gratefully.

He rushed up the stairs.

On the first floor there were three doors; one was the bathroom, the other two were bedrooms. The floor moved

Luke James

beneath his feet; the foundations of the house beginning to crumble and burn away beneath. One wall of the house was turning black, as though there was a fire on the other side.

Clasping his bleeding arm, he ran into the biggest bedroom and finally saw his prize: a red, retro-style phone on the bedside table.

Every nerve in his body began to shake. Would this actually work? What if it didn't?

He picked up the phone and perched on the side of the double bed. Timidly, he brought it to his ear, afraid he would hear nothing but silence.

Struggling to believe it when he heard the dial tone, he pulled the phone away again, testing whether the faint buzz was coming from the earpiece. It faded, lost amongst the cracking walls and failing floorboards.

Flying debris burst through the roof of the house, falling through the ceiling and tearing a hole through the bedroom floor just a few feet away from him.

Within the hole the raptor leapt up, snapping its jaws. But it couldn't reach. Tucking the phone under his arm, Norman pulled the bedside table away from wall and nudged it into the hole.

It smashed to pieces as it landed on the raptor's head, instantly subduing the monster.

Norman put the phone back to his ear, and the hum returned. He closed his eyes and took a breath.

Fighting to ignore the house collapsing beneath him and the prehistoric beast trying to snap at his feet, he dialled the number to the landline of the house he shared with Fury in the real world.

After a lingering breath, the phone rang.

CHAPTER SEVENTEEN

The model railway no longer looked like a model railway, but an angry teenager's torture table for the forgotten toys of their youth, all innocence discarded, replaced with angst and disappointment at the psychotic realities of adult life. The surface was burnt and scalded with noxious chemicals like a science experiment gone-wrong. Bent and broken toys lay scattered across the surface – a graveyard where no one was left alive to dig the holes.

The room was dark. If it was day outside, the blackout curtains kept it a secret. Through tired eyes Fury could still see Norman's gentle glow over by the crushed toy buildings and the spilt sodium bicarbonate and vinegar she'd used for the lava. He was alive. But he wouldn't be for long.

She should probably intervene, shouldn't she? Hell and Earth had merged in her mind and it wasn't clear what the rules were anymore. The damned souls were already dead by the time they got to her pit, their chance of a living redemption blown out. But Norman was still alive. Still reprievable - wasn't he? Did she even want to forgive him? There was no judge here to determine whether his penance was up.

Where was her mother? She could have sworn she smelled her smoky presence lingering nearby. Or was that from all the things she'd burned in bringing chaos to the model world? She hadn't been around for a few days – not since Norman's betrayal. How many days had it been?

Model Railway Apocalypse

Fury lay her horned head down on the surface, as if listening for answers to all these questions. She closed her eyes.

These days everyone wanted to be a torturer. It meant there was a surplus. Being a custodian used to be a prestigious position, but more and more Fury felt like it was losing kudos. Even with the astronomical increase in damnation over the last hundred years, she'd often found herself waiting around for long periods before a new soul arrived into her custody. This resulted in Fury keeping her pit immaculately tidy. Pokers and paddles hung straight on their hooks, while the whips and chains were neatly coiled and ready for use. The torture table was virtually stain-free and the ground was nearly always clear of human waste.

On this particular day Fury sat on the edge of her table, dangling her long legs, waiting for something to happen. Surely there was some recently deceased scumbag in need of penance. She could really go to town on a serial killer or a snuff producer about now. She was in that kind of mood. This time she would go slowly. She wouldn't be so quick to hand him or her over to the judges. She reminded herself to savour each soul, sipping it as if it was a long drink rather than impetuously downing it like a shot. The judges had told her she was becoming a bit too efficient.

"It's missing the point," they'd said. Fury couldn't help that she was good at her job.

She withdrew the knife from her boot and used it to further emboss some of the tally marks on the table. She was nearly up to sixty-thousand now.

As she blew away the excess sawdust, the giant colon above her pit started to wobble and groan. She looked up

Luke James

and saw the human-sized lump working its way to the aperture.

With a squirty fart noise her next victim popped out and landed on the soft membrane floor of her pit.

A male. Early sixties. He lay naked in the foetal position, his skin shiny from his journey through the infernal intestine. He had his back to her, and remained curled up.

She prodded him with her boot. He unfurled and turned to face her.

"Who are you?" he asked, like a child on his first day of school.

Slightly unusual first impression, she noted. Usually they appeared a little more alarmed.

"I'm Fury," she answered. "You'll be in my charge for a while."

She grabbed him by the arm and pulled him to his feet. He didn't resist for a second, actually seeming grateful for the assistance. Neither did he struggle as she dragged him across the pit and lifted him onto the table.

"Wow. People are physical around here," he said.

She grimaced, trying to appear threatening.

"Lie flat," she told him.

"Where is here, exactly?" he asked while she took each of his limbs and fixed them to the four corners of her torture table.

"Haven't you worked it out yet?" She smiled. "You're in Hell."

"I suspected as much," he said with a sigh. His shoulders slumped and he glanced at his surroundings.

Why isn't he more afraid? Usually by this point, they were panicking and thrashing like a fish on a coffee table. Why is he so different? What has he done?

"May I ask what for?" he asked.

111

Model Railway Apocalypse

"That's what I'm about to find out. Put your head back."

He obliged, letting her place a strap over his forehead. She pulled it tight so he couldn't lift his head. Then she placed her hand on his head and looked into his soul.

Sin-searching was part of the job Fury always found fascinating. What had they done? What secrets did they keep? It was her favourite form of story-telling – shining a spotlight into someone's essence, looking for shadows. What would she find? She enjoyed the sense of discovery. Would she uncover an original sin? They were rare, but in the modern day they did happen.

"I'm Jeremy," he said, interrupting her examination. "It's nice to meet you, Fury. I'd shake your hand but... well...." He gestured towards the restraints on his wrists.

"Be quiet."

"Sorry."

The search was proving difficult. Whatever he'd done it was well hidden, deep beneath the surface. He must be one nasty bastard, she thought as she continued rummaging. She was eager to get to work.

"Anything, yet?" he asked after a few moments.

She didn't answer. She merely frowned and kept feeling around inside his spirit.

Something wasn't right. No matter how hard she looked, she couldn't find anything. There were a couple of petty crimes in his youth and a speeding offence in his mid-twenties, but nothing worthy of damnation. Eventually she stopped searching and asked him directly.

"Any idea why you might be here?"

He shrugged. "I never went to church," he said. "Does that count?"

"No, actually. Anything else?"

"I didn't spend enough time with my son."

Luke James

Fury shook her head, becoming frustrated. She needed a second opinion.

"Wait here," she said, climbing out of the pit, leaving him strapped to the torture table.

"No problem," he said.

She didn't know how long the phone had been ringing or how long she'd been asleep. A few seconds, or a few hours? She opened her eyes and lifted her head. A glance at the model told her Norman was still alive, but he hadn't moved.

The ringing came from the next room, the master bedroom. She stood up and went to pick it up. She entered the bedroom she shared with Norman, hesitating when she began to wonder who could be calling.

Daylight pooled into the room through the open curtains. A glance at the clock on her bedside table told her it was 8am.

Who could it be? The obvious answer was Malice, though she didn't tend to call so early. Fury's legs became stiff at the thought of speaking to her daughter. No doubt she'd ask about her dad. What would she say? Weren't Malice and Henry supposed to be visiting soon? What day was it?

Fury perched on the side of the marital bed to contemplate. She hadn't been able to bring herself to sleep in the bed since he'd betrayed her.

The answer machine clicked in. The receiver message played. Fury was startled to hear the recording of Norman's warm, familiar voice. Hello, we can't come to the phone right now. Please leave a message after the beep. The recording was cheerful and to the point.

The machine beeped.

Model Railway Apocalypse

At first there as only crackling, like white noise on the line. Then breathing. Her whole body shivered when she heard him.

"Angel...please."

She heard a sniff.

Could it be?

"Please..."

The familiar voice. The warmth.

"...give me a chance to explain."

More breathing. More crackling – louder this time.

"That's all I ask."

Her eyes welled up, warmed by fiery tears beneath.

"Please."

The machine clicked off.

Burying her head in her hands, she wailed.

Fury returned to the spare room and examined the anarchy. She wiped away the fluids and the hazards surrounding Norman, and considered what to do next.

He hadn't apologised. Not even grovelled. What of that?

He was still alive, she knew that much. In his message he sounded distressed, but not angry. Other than that she didn't know what kind of state he was in.

What about her? She went to the hallway mirror and saw herself – tired, teary eyed, demonic. She couldn't go to him like that.

A chance to explain? Okay then.

Something wasn't right. Ferocity perched on the wall, watching through eight unblinking eyes while her daughter wiped tears from her face. It had been many decades since she'd seen Fury cry. Who had been on the phone? Why had she undone her good work on the miniature world?

Luke James

Unable to tell what Fury was thinking, she descended her web to get a better look.

Something definitely wasn't right. Ferocity felt nervous that her web was about to unravel. Her daughter's return to her was under threat.

Fury stood up and left the room.

Ferocity crawled along the walls, following as her daughter walked into the master bedroom. She perched in the archway of the door, watching Fury open the wardrobe and throw dress after dress on the bed.

Fury's beautiful blue skin was fading back into that sickly hue of human skin. It can't be, Ferocity thought, her eight legs tensing as horror set in. She's going to him.

Fury sat down at her dressing table and reached for her make-up.

No, no, no. Ferocity fumed inside. This cannot be allowed to happen.

Luke James

CHAPTER EIGHTEEN

The street was quiet now. The world was at peace. Calm carnage still lay dormant about the town and the air hummed with the kind of catharsis common after waking from a nightmare. It even felt lighter now, like morning was about to break. Norman walked through the narrow street where lava no longer flowed, through the skeleton of a town savaged by an angry Goddess.

He hoped this all meant she'd heard. But hope was dangerous.

He'd wrapped his shoulder in an old jumper found in the room where he'd made the phone call, tying it tightly to put pressure on the wound raptor had left him.

As he cleared the buildings, he saw the robot lying collapsed on the green, next to the fallen giantess. He searched the scene for Baz and Julie, hoping they were still alive. He called out their names and waited.

There was no sign of his companions. No sign of anyone left living. He turned his eyes to the ground, accepting that maybe he should be looking for their bodies instead.

If she'd heard, why wasn't she here yet?

Now he was completely alone. There wasn't even an echo as he called for his new friends. He walked across the park, regarding the chaos, the dead soldiers and dinosaurs, the fallen robot and giant woman. Although the ground was still covered in ash, the air felt clearer. He could breathe deeply without his lungs punishing him. There was a buzzing noise behind him. He turned around

Model Railway Apocalypse

and saw a ball of iridescent blue light hovering a meter off the ground. It flickered with electricity and cast itself into a familiar form. The light dissipated and there she was, looking radiant.

She's here. He couldn't believe it. She's really here. Norman fell to his knees, ignoring the burning ash as it dug into his skin. She walked towards him, wearing a pale blue dress with a sunflower pattern, and make-up on her frowning face.

"Thank you," he said, looking up at her. "Thank you for giving me a chance to explain."

"That's why I'm here," she said.

He could see the hurt in her eyes. The needless hurt she'd been carrying.

"It was your mother," he said. "She tricked me."

"What do you mean?" she asked.

"She got to me just before you did. At the bed and breakfast."

"She was here?" she said, shaking her head. There was anger in her voice.

He nodded.

"She'd shifted to look just like you. I thought she was you. That's why when she kissed me, I kissed her back. I thought I was kissing my wife. But then I looked up and saw you standing in the door, and she'd turned again – into that barmaid."

She tilted her head, reflecting on what he'd said.

"You've got to believe me. I thought she was you."

Tears filled his eyes as he looked deep into hers.

"I wouldn't do that to you, Fury. Please believe me."

As he said her name, she put her hands in his hair, running her fingers through it. Her touch was ethereal.

Luke James

He'd missed it so much.

"Do you?"

"Do I what?

"Do you believe me?"

She placed her hands either side of his face, as though she was thinking about kissing him. He hesitated, wanting to know that she trusted him first. Kissing her without that didn't seem right.

He remembered the flowers in his pocket, the ones he'd been carrying all this time. He reached in and presented them to her. They were withered and only a few petals were left intact. It felt like a pathetic gesture, but he'd held onto them for this long.

"Tell me you do," he said.

She looked at the flowers, but didn't take them.

Fury had once told him about a pour soul who ended up in Hell when he clearly wasn't meant to be there. She told him about how she had recognised something different about this man. He hadn't responded to the threat of torture in the usual way – none of the anger or guilt or sorrow shown by the usual tenants of Hell, just a clear despondency. He carried the weight of innocence, not the curse of guilt. Norman sincerely hoped she recognised it in him now.

With a smile, she took his hands in hers and pulled him to his feet.

"I believe you, my dear," she said, wiping a tear from his cheek with her thumb.

She kissed him.

Norman heard the air buzzing again as he kissed her back. He kept his eyes closed. When he opened his eyes, would they appear back in the spare room? She pressed

Model Railway Apocalypse

her lips against his forcefully, wrapping her arms around him and pulling his body tightly against hers. He even felt her fingers digging into his back, like they were clawing at his spine.

When he opened his eyes she was watching him, smiling.

She pulled him in again, forcing his lips against hers. She tasted minty. The air around them continued to crackle with electricity, the same way it had before she'd appeared.

Something's not right.

She was smirking, laughing as she kissed him.

Norman pulled himself away, fighting against the rigid grip of her hands.

When he finally managed to release himself form her grip, his worst fears were confirmed. The woman he was kissing wasn't his wife, but his mother-in-law posing as the flirty, full-chested barmaid from before.

Wait... the buzzing air... Fury!

He looked over the woman's shoulder and saw her. The real her. His wife. The love of his life. Looking on. Devastated once again.

Fury no longer recognised this man who was supposed to be her husband. Is this why he wanted her to come?

She exploded into her demon form and struck the slutty barmaid with a quick, sharp burst of magic from her tail. The barmaid flew backwards, landing on the ashen ground, instantly losing consciousness.

Fury glared at Norman, who looked at the woman lying on the floor, as if more concerned about the welfare of the tart than her.

"Wait!" he shouted.

How dare he raise his voice? Who is he to make demands

Luke James

of me ever again?

Even though she'd left, she always carried Hell inside her, deep inside her chest. Now it was flaring up and spreading through her veins. It grasped her like an old friend reunited.

Norman ran towards her.

She raised her tail, and pointed it at him.

"Don't come any closer," she warned.

He ignored her. She fired a bolt of magic from her tail and struck him in the chest.

Luke James

CHAPTER NINETEEN

The ground was hot and coarse against Norman's face. His wounded shoulder pulsated beneath him. He fought the urge to close his eyes and surrender to his fate. Maybe he'd wake up and find it had just been a really bad dream. More likely he wouldn't, but if he didn't wake up at all it would be better than what was happening to him right now.

He drifted in and out of consciousness. The Hellish soundscape of thunder, flames and shrieking drifted closer and further away as though someone was twisting a volume control up and down. Maybe he was already dead. Perhaps he'd had a heart attack while building the model railway and this was the afterlife.

"Norman," said a nearby voice.

He couldn't be sure if his eyes were open or closed. The nightmare visions were the same either way.

"Buddy, can you hear me?" The voice was familiar, but the low-key, solemn tone was alien. He felt himself rocking, unsure whether someone was jostling him or if it was the ground moving once again. When he finally opened his eyes, he saw it was both.

Baz sat next to him, his large body as still as a rock despite the quivering ground.

Norman sat upright, glad to see his friend alive. Something was wrong, though. Baz gazed at the ground. His baby-face looked fatigued, as if his spirit had been sedated.

Their surroundings were hidden by a mist, which

Model Railway Apocalypse

circled around them, not that Baz seemed to notice. Beyond it the screams continued – someone was still alive in this world other than the two of them.

There was no sign of Fury. Nor was there any sign of the barmaid – or Ferocity posing as the barmaid. Had Fury killed her - her own mother - without realising who she was? He doubted Ferocity would let that happen. The flowers lay on the ground beside him, the last of the petals withered black.

"Did it work?" Baz asked, as though the answer didn't really matter.

"It did," Norman said, shattered.

"Didn't go so well, hey?" Baz asked, though it was more a statement.

"Not exactly. Where's Julie?" Norman asked, suddenly noting her absence.

Baz hung his head.

"Didn't make it," he said.

"What happened?"

"We got away from the robot, and managed to hide in the giant lady's cleavage. We sat tight until things went quiet. Eventually I looked out and saw the robot lying on the ground. We figured your plan had worked. That the nightmares had gone away. We couldn't believe it. We danced and yelled and celebrated. Julie wanted to wash off the coal and ash so she ran into the river."

He winced, staring down at his empty hands, which were glowing red, much of the skin on them burnt away.

"I should have seen it sooner... The noxious gases swirling above the water... The toxic waste sign... The hulking factory with its leaking concrete pipes....

"When she realised what was happening to her... the river digesting her... like a piece of meat. I tried to reach

Luke James

for her. Tried to pull her out, but she fell to pieces in my hands. I didn't know a person could melt like that."

His eyes were red with tears.

"I couldn't do it. I couldn't save her."

Norman felt a scratching in his throat. He watched as snot and tears mixed together on Baz's face. The big man sniffed and trembled. Norman tucked his hand inside his sleeve, and used the cuff of his robe to wipe his friend's nose.

"Thanks," Baz said, grabbing the sleeve and blowing his nose on it.

"You're welcome," Norman said. "I'm sorry."

"How'd it go with your wife?" Baz asked, still blinking back his tears.

"Could have gone better, I must say."

"Crying shame!" Baz beamed. "You need to hold on to her tightly, Norman..." he said blowing his nose again. "You never know when you're going to lose her."

"I think I already have. I'm not sure how I'm going to get her back now."

"There's always a way, buddy," Baz said, putting his arm on Norman's bad shoulder. Norman winced.

"Shit! What happened to you?"

"Got bitten by a raptor," Norman said.

"Can't leave you alone for a minute!"

Norman shook his head. "I swatted it with a wooden spoon," he said. He couldn't help but smiled to himself. "Then a saucepan."

Baz smirked.

It did sound pretty ridiculous, Norman supposed.

"At least we've got eachother," Baz said with a smile.

"True. I thought I was all alone."

"No one's ever alone; at worst you're only two people

Model Railway Apocalypse

short of a threesome."

The large man's belly jiggled as he started to giggle. Before he knew what was happening, Norman found himself laughing too. With all this madness and devastation, what else was there to do?

Falling over had been easy, as had pretending to be unconscious long enough for the others to become distracted. Slipping away unnoticed was even easier.

The blast of magic from her daughter hadn't hurt her in the slightest. She still kept Fury's secret, and that kept her safe from her powers. If anything, the attack had given her a feeling of warmth, radiating through her body, to see her Fury unleash those powers. How she'd slid effortlessly back into her beautiful demonic form. How naturally her eyes had glowed with wrath. Ferocity was a proud mother.

What does a spider do when its web is getting frail? Simply add another knot or two. She felt a tingling in her chest as she skittered away. Soon her daughter would come back to her.

She exited the miniature world and perched back on the wall, getting an arachnid's-eye view of the spare room. She just had to wait it out now - wait until Fury came out, needing maternal comfort.

Soon though, impatience got the better of her. There was no sign of Fury; she'd stayed inside the model.

Sitting around twitching her eight legs wasn't as interesting as viewing first-hand the mayhem her daughter was probably letting loose on that contemptable husband of hers. Ick, had she really kissed him? Twice? She swallowed down a bit of spider sick.

Ferocity wanted to get a better look at the action. She shot a thread up to the ceiling and climbed until she

Luke James

was directly above the model. Then she lowered herself, summoning her magic to transport herself into the miniature world.

This was going to be fun.

Fury walked among the bodies and rubble. There was a striking difference between sitting at the side, watching the flickering on the surface, and being immersed in the mire of madness she'd nurtured. From demon to goddess of her very own dominion, there was something depressing about being able to create life and destroy it so easily. She felt a sense of responsibility for the tiny lives she'd forged while bringing joy to her husband. Their shells lay around the decaying town, sacrificed as collateral in her bid to punish him. Some still groaned, as though they knew their creator - and tormentor - was nearby.

A little way down the hill, the mist still gathered. Up on the peak, the eruption had resumed. The fires she'd summoned, as if directly from Hell, were scattered around, just to make it feel a little more like home.

In no hurry to leave, she could make this her garden for a while; it was named after her after all.

A hand grabbed her leg, just above the boot. She looked down at the unfortunate individual: a young man. His bloodshot eyes gazed up at her as if pleading for relief. Fury crouched down and ran her hand over his cheek. He shuddered beneath her touch. She stood up and walked on.

Why hadn't she done this sooner? Playing God was more interesting when you were able to walk among your handiwork. Of course, she knew why she'd kept out of the miniature world: she had to find a way to deal with her

Model Railway Apocalypse

tangled feelings for Norman without having to face him in person. Remodelling was a non-direct, more subtle approach than the outright offensive her demon-kind might have condoned.

But now it was different. He'd betrayed her. Then he'd lured her back to wound her a second time. She owed him a few wounds in return.

She elevated her tail and the bodies around her began to rise.

The mist continued to circle Norman and Baz as they sat in the ash. It closed in around them, making it impossible to see further than a train-car-length in any direction. It was as if the world was ending, falling away, getting smaller and smaller before it disappeared into oblivion and there'd be nothing left to stand on - nothing left to breathe. The screams seeping through the mist neither confirmed nor refuted that possibility.

"Did you see my wife?" Norman asked.

"I saw someone running away up the hill, but I couldn't make out any detail."

"Running away?" Norman was surprised at the phrasing. "You mean she didn't disappear?"

"Disappear?" Baz seemed confused.

"Yeah. As in vanish into thin air?"

"No, buddy. Whoever it was ran off up that way," he said pointing towards the town. "In quite a hurry, from what I could tell. Like I say, I couldn't see any detail, just a shadow disappearing into the mist. I suppose in a way they did disappear."

"But not into thin air?"

"No." Baz shook his head. "Why?"

The fact that he had seen someone running was

Luke James

significant; it meant whoever it was - Fury or Ferocity - hadn't simply exited the world. That meant there was a chance they were still here. If Fury was still around then he had to get to her. It might be his only chance to make things right.

But what if it turned out to be Ferocity? He'd worry about that at the time. Finding Fury was worth the risk.

"Which way did they go?" Norman asked.

Baz pointed up the hill towards the town, which was hidden by the mist.

"We need to find them," Norman said, scrambling to his feet. Baz followed suit.

"Don't forget these," the large man said, picking up the dead flowers and handing them to Norman.

"Thanks," Norman said. He would be embarrassed to give the deceased hyacinths to Fury now, but he nodded gratefully anyway, and put them back in his robe pocket. When he looked up in the direction of the town, a mass of shadows was shambling towards them through the mist.

Luke James

CHAPTER TWENTY

The contorted bodies shuffled awkwardly, their glowing red eyes illuminating the mist like car headlights on a deserted road. It was clear these were the dead locals reanimated, but even Norman could tell, their fuse wasn't lit by the same spark as it had been before. They had small horns protruding from their heads, and their faces were angry. These weren't human anymore, but demonic creatures fuelled by Hell's fire.

"What do we do?" Baz asked.

"I'm open to suggestions." Norman swallowed as the demonites moved closer. "Still got that gun?"

Baz shook his head.

"Lost it running from the robot."

Although the creatures moved awkwardly, taking them on in a brawl was the last thing Norman wanted, especially given their sheer numbers and the numbness in his arm from the raptor bite. Baz - on the other hand - raised his fists, getting ready for a punch-up.

Ever the optimist, Norman observed.

He remembered the bread knife in his robe pocket, but cutting into angry dead people wasn't his idea of a good time.

"Let's run," he said.

"Thank God," Baz muttered as the two of them turned and ran in the opposite direction.

The horde followed.

131

Model Railway Apocalypse

Many fell behind, but the more athletic monsters kept up with little difficulty.

Norman had never been a natural runner, and Baz didn't seem like he was in contention for a gold medal. They couldn't run forever, and they were moving in the wrong direction if he wanted to get to Fury.

They needed to find a way to lose the living dead, preferably without having to fight their way through them.

Up ahead he saw the train station. Could they board a train and leave the horde behind? He remembered the psychotic train that had tried to mow him down. The alternative was to head towards the river, maybe leap over it and hope the demonites were stupid enough to fall in and melt.

It was a split-second decision: he'd rather take his chances with Thomas the Tank Engine's sadistic big brother than risk falling into the toxic river himself.

"I've got an idea," Norman said, adjusting his direction towards the station. Baz followed suit.

They ran through the station house, closing the door on their pursuers and pulling a metal bin in front of it. It wouldn't hold them up more than a few seconds, but it would buy them time as they ran along the platform where the locomotive still sat, trailed by six carriages.

"Dude, you're back!" the large train peeped when they reached the front.

"Yes," Norman said.

Baz gave him a perturbed look.

"Oh yeah," Norman said. "He talks."

Baz put his hands up in the air, as if to say: I'm not going to argue.

Glass smashed as the demonites broke through the

Luke James

door of the station house and spilled onto the platform.

"Here's the deal," Norman said. "We're going to put the loco-path shenanigans to one side. We're going to climb aboard and you're going to get us out of here. Deal?"

"Dude-dude!" the train peeped. Black smoke wafted through its funnel. "All aboard if you want to live!"

Norman and Baz climbed into the cabin and the locomotive shot out of the station.

"Surf steel boys!" the train chirped as it continued to pick up speed with Norman and Baz holding on in the cabin. They seemed to be clear of the creatures, who ran to the end of the platform, watching them disappear out of reach.

"We lost 'em!" Baz said.

"That's good." Norman took a moment to catch his breath. He needed to get to Fury. The train would circle around, passing by the town - or what used to be the town - before entering the tunnels beneath the hill. He could get the locomotive to stop and drop them off.

Norman didn't know what to call the train. Its name was The Phoenix, but he wasn't sure it would respond to that.

"Er...dude?" he said, improvising.

"Yeah, little dude?" the train replied instantly.

"Do you mind—"

A heavy weight came down on Norman from behind. He fell to the floor of the cabin, smacking his face against the hard surface. Hands grabbed either side of his head and squeezed his skull.

"What's that dude?" the train asked, picking up speed.

Norman cried out. The pressure on his head was getting unbearable. Then it was gone. He looked up to see Baz throwing the attacking demonite off the train.

The large man offered his hand, which Norman accepted

133

Model Railway Apocalypse

gratefully. Before he could stand, three more creatures leapt down into the cabin, two landing on Baz's back, dragging him to the ground. They'd somehow made it on to the train before it was clear of the station.

"What's going on back there?" the train rumbled.

Norman scrambled to his feet, finding himself face-to-face with one of the scowling demonites. Its skin had a bluish hue, much like Fury's, although this creature was ugly. It had sharp teeth and pointed claws. Norman noticed the dog tags hanging around his neck. One of the soldiers, he realised, as it punched him in the face, knocking him backwards. He fought to keep his footing as the ex-soldier lashed at him again, this time scratching his face with its sharp claws.

Norman cried out, feeling warmth as blood ran down his cheek. He wasn't a violent person, but being clawed in the face seemed to stoke his ire. He found a handle to steady himself then threw his leg forwards, kicking the demonite between its legs. It groaned, clutching itself and looking Norman in the eye as if to say: that was low.

Norman nodded, then jabbed his foot forward again, this time hitting the creature's chest. It fell backwards and out of the cabin.

Baz was still wrestling with the other two creatures on the floor of the cab. He lay across one, pinning it down while the other lay on top of him, pulling his hair.

"Brace yourselves, dudes!" the train called out through the thick air. "We're about to turn the heat up!"

Norman glanced out of the cabin. They'd already passed the town. He'd missed his chance to get to Fury, for now anyway. He looked forwards and saw what the train's warning was about: they were approaching the tunnel beneath the peak that had previously transformed into

134

Luke James

the volcano. Norman shuddered as it appeared to have resumed its terrible eruption.

"What are you doing?" he snapped at the train.

"What can I say, dude? I'm an experientialist! Hang on!"

Norman gulped, ducking under the canopy of the cab as they shot through the spraying lava-waterfall and into the glowing red tunnel.

"A little help here would be great," Baz said, still tussling with the pair of demonites. Now they were both on top of him, one kneeling on his legs, the other on his head.

Norman grabbed an iron bar, which was hanging inside of the cab. He guessed it was a poker - used to tend the coal inside the furnace. He, however, used it to crack one of the demonites around the back of the head.

It fell forwards instantly, lifting its knee from Baz's head. Norman swung the rod at the other, but the creature grabbed it with two hands. It snarled at him. This one, too, wore dogtags.

Norman remembered the breadknife in his pocket. He grabbed it and sliced at the creature's wrists. Its hands maintained their tight grip on the iron bar, but they were no longer attached to the creature's arms. Its hellish scream filled the inside of the fiery volcano as it stared in disbelief at the stumps where its hands use to be.

Such a crude weapon, Norman thought as he slid the knife back into his pocket. The severed hands slid of the iron rod as he seized it again, using it to pelt the demonite around the head. It fell off Baz's legs. With a little kick, it fell out of the train and into a lava pool inside the volcano.

The inside of the volcano was exactly how Norman imagined Hell to be: red rocks, flaring fires and spraying lava.

Baz was back on his feet, exchanging punches with the final demonite. Norman raised the rod again and swung it

Model Railway Apocalypse

at the creature.

A wave of lava sprayed over the cab.

"Oh, that tickles!" said the train.

Norman ducked down under the canopy, but Baz was too slow. A fat splash of lava spilled onto his arm, instantly incinerating the limb from the shoulder down. The large man didn't even cry out. He simply lost consciousness and collapsed to the floor.

"Whoooop!" whistled the train.

Norman was left alone with the creature, who'd also managed to dodge the spray of lava. Around them - and inside them - the fires of Hell burned while lung-melting fumes made each breath feel like a step closer to death.

The final creature leapt at him, knocking him backwards and pinning him to the floor so that his head hung precariously out of the cabin. Norman turned to see the large wheels of the locomotive rotate furiously as it surged through the volcano. Up ahead a stream of lava dripped down beside the track. If he didn't move, it would soon be dripping down on his head.

The demonite growled as it held him in its grip. He recognised the belligerent face and the silver hair. The Major, back for revenge.

He knew it was a bad idea – he'd done it once before and it hadn't worked out so well – but it was the only move Norman had left: he nutted the demon Major as hard as he could.

Both of them groaned at the impact, although it probably hurt Norman more – he'd forgotten about the small horns on the demon's crown, which left little dents in his forehead and more warm blood running down his face.

The move, while regrettable, hadn't been entirely pointless. The demonite had inadvertently loosened

Luke James

its grip, allowing Norman to roll out from beneath it. He tucked his head into the cabin before it was melted off by the stream of lava.

He tried to stand up but the creature grabbed his legs, tripping him over, falling forwards into the cabin.

"Need more coal, dude!" the train called out.

An arm's length in front of him the small iron door to the firebox popped open, and a rush of heat blasted at Norman's face.

He rolled onto his back as the Major, now with blood-soaked horns, lurched towards him. Norman threw his feet into the air to shield himself. The creature ran into him, taking swipes at his face with its sharp claws.

Norman saw his chance. He used his legs to pivot the demonite over the top of him, throwing it towards the open furnace. The Major fell head-first into the flames. His body went into spasm, shrieks echoing inside the furnace. Norman had to turn away until he finally fell still.

"Oh, that's the stuff!" the train said, exiting the tunnel beneath the volcano. "We made it – what a rush!"

Norman hurried to the side of his fallen friend who was still unconscious but not bleeding. The raw stump of his arm had been cauterised by the lava.

The train would circle back past the town before arriving back at the station.

"Stop just up here," Norman shouted at the train.

"Had enough, dude?"

"Just do it!"

The train screeched and squealed on the steel rails as it ground to a halt just before crossing the bridge above the toxic river.

It was just a short walk to the town from here.

Luke James

CHAPTER TWENTY-ONE

With Baz's remaining arm draped over him, Norman trudged towards the town, trying hard to keep moving under the large man's weight. Baz had stirred shortly after the train stopped, waking up just enough to take some of the strain as they alighted. Although he'd thanked the locomotive for helping them, Norman couldn't shake off the chill he'd felt at the train's last words, spoken as he and Baz hobbled away from the tracks: "See you shortly, dude," he'd said, blowing off reams of steam.

As they got closer to town, Baz took back more and more of his own weight. Norman was desperate to find Fury, but he wasn't going to leave his friend behind.

"Come on, raptor-slayer," he said, trying to encourage Baz along. "We're nearly there."

There weren't any demonites around here, but Norman figured they'd be back soon enough.

Ahead of them, mist still lay over the town like a duvet. There were fires scattered around the ruins, like candles at a vigil. The only evidence that Fury had been there was that the dilapidated buildings had been pulled apart and put back together, reassembled into looming industrial structures. There was a theme of steel and iron and smoke, chimneys and factories and towers. The air was pulsing with hot air and fumes.

They walked past a sign which once cheerfully read: "Welcome to Furydale!" The "dale" had been crossed out and replaced with "hell".

Model Railway Apocalypse

Despite the grimness of the scene, Norman felt uplifted by the idea that Fury had been here – it meant she was probably nearby.

He picked up the pace, which became easier as Baz supported himself more and more.

Ferocity kept her distance, watching her daughter refashion the clumsy human town. She'd brought Hell to this place; eventually, she'd realise it was no substitute for the real thing. Let her enjoy herself, Ferocity thought. She'll be home soon.

She could see the logic behind her daughter's behaviour. Having spent so long abiding human customs, she had to surround herself with a bit of homely Hell in order to condition herself to do what any demon would do – to do what needed to be done.

Somewhere in the distance a train whistled. Fury stood up and scanned the horizon. Ferocity hid behind one of the new structures. If Fury saw her now, everything would be ruined. She'd sent an army of creatures after that pathetic husband.

But it seemed to Ferocity that something wasn't going to plan.

Fury made herself grow huge. Why not? This was her world. Why not make herself a leviathan? She stood as tall as a town house. Armoured and ready to kill, Ferocity watched her walk away into the mist. She couldn't help but be a proud mother; one way or another, today she'd see the end of the human Norman.

And here he comes now...

When walking among them, the industrial structures were far bigger than they seemed on the horizon. Wire

Luke James

and bars wrapped around grey apartment blocks and a black brick prison. Norman heard the crack of a whips on an industrial scale, followed by waves of screams.

"Fury!" he called out, scanning the demon streets for his wife.

"Fury?" Baz echoed. "That's her name?"

"Yeah," Norman said. "It's a demon name."

"I like it," Baz said, gesturing towards the small fires. "Suits her perfectly."

In places there were stringy bits of something silky - something that shimmered in the firelight. It hung between some of the buildings like washing lines. It made Norman nervous.

Baz had reached out with his remaining arm and grabbed some of the silky substance.

"Wait!" Norman shouted. But it was too late.

"It's sticky," he said. He tried to run his hand along it, but it wouldn't move. He tried to pull it away but the whole strand became taut.

"I can't let go!" Baz said. "My hand is stuck!"

Norman took hold of his arm and helped him tug, but the harder they pulled the more rigid the strand became.

"Help me!" Baz started taking panicked breaths and thrashing his arm around erratically. He'd already been through enough trauma losing two girlfriends and his arm.

Once again, Norman remembered the knife in his pocket. He didn't like carrying it, but in this world it felt necessary. With a simple slice, he cut through the strand, setting Baz's hand free again. It still had a bit of the silky stuff stuck to it, but at least he wasn't attached to the larger line any more.

Norman re-sheathed the knife in his robe and tried

141

Model Railway Apocalypse

to console his friend, who crouched down on the floor, groaning to himself like a broken man.

"You're okay," Norman assured him, though he knew it was futile. After what Baz had been through, he couldn't blame him for falling apart. He didn't know what else to say.

But they weren't okay. A large shadow fell over them. It had eight legs and eight eyes and was the size of a house.

"We're not okay," Norman whispered to Baz. The large man was oblivious, still bawling his eyes out in his hands.

"Baz, Baz, Baz, Baz..." Norman said tapping him on the shoulder repeatedly. "We need to move."

"Huh?" Baz finally looked up at the monster, black and shiny with sharp fangs the size of human arms. Then he was off, leaving Norman in a cloud of dust.

Fury towered above her demonites who gathered at the station. As she approached, they knelt down, murmuring between themselves.

She raised her hand and they fell silent.

"It's not your fault, my darlings. You were ill-equipped for the task."

Fury elevated her tail, so it pointed over her shoulder like a cannon.

"It won't happen again," she said. She shot a beam of magic over the kneeling crowd.

Screams filled the air as their backs rippled and reshaped. The skin on their shoulder blades split open and new appendages burst out, growing longer and longer. They fanned out, thin leathery skin hung down, veins visible.

"Rise, my dark angels," Fury commanded.

Bat-like shrieks replaced the screams as the creatures

Luke James

stood and flapped their wings, thrusting into the air. All of them became airborne, but one. The barmaid remained on the ground. She was still completely human. Her hands were tied.

Luke James

CHAPTER TWENTY-TWO

Fleeing through the demonic industrial town, pursued by the giant spider, Norman and Baz were quickly running out of breath.

When he looked back over his shoulder Norman noticed the giant arachnid was neither losing nor gaining on them. It was simply maintaining a consistent distance. Given its size it was difficult to believe it wasn't able to catch them.

Soon he became convinced that the eight-legged monster was just trying to mess with them.

This was confirmed when a familiar smirk came from behind – a deep, female voice, rattling between steel structures.

Norman glanced behind him again. He was met with the eight beady eyes right in his face – alien and grotesque. Could this thing be his mother-in-law? She'd spent his entire marriage trying to intimidate and sabotage him. After everything, it made sense that if there was a way to kill him, she'd take it.

If this was Ferocity then where was Fury? Had she already left the world? Was it Ferocity who Baz had seen running through the mist towards the town?

A sense of hopelessness overcame him. His legs and his lungs gave up working and he dropped back.

"What are you doing?" Baz asked looking over his shoulder.

"It's pointless," Norman mumbled, more to himself.

Baz halted his running.

145

Model Railway Apocalypse

The giant spider arched over Norman and thrust a leg forwards, impaling Baz through the stomach.

"Baz!" Norman yelled, watching on in terror. No, no, no!

The large man didn't make any noise. Screaming was beyond him as she pinned him to the ground, lurching over him, smirking again.

"You're finally accepting the truth," the spider gloated. There was no longer any doubt in Norman's mind: this was Ferocity.

Norman ran to the large man's side. The spider didn't move, laughing as she kept her leg inside Baz's torso.

Norman knew she was doing this to hurt him. She was torturing him by maiming his friend. He'd probably be next. Would she really go that far and risk being disowned by her daughter? Or was Fury somewhere nearby letting this happen?

Blood oozed out of Baz's stomach. Ferocity wiggled her leg around inside the wound, cackling. Baz gurgled.

Norman removed the breadknife from his pocket. In one swift movement he slashed through the giant leg implanted in his friend.

Ferocity shrieked. Thick black blood gushed from the top of her leg. She stumbled backwards, lifting the stump up and inspecting it with her eight beady eyes. Norman swung again, slicing off another leg.

She backed away. Something was changing in her now. Her spider form seemed to be melting, shrinking, changing from black to blue. She was returning to her demon self.

When the transformation was complete, she was hunched over gawking at her hands. Norman noticed digits missing from each one.

Instinctively he stepped towards her, as most people would with someone who was injured. But he remembered

Luke James

what she'd done to Baz. And what she'd done to him. She'd framed him. Everything that had happened here was because of her.

She looked up at him through pained red eyes. He took another step towards her, but before he could make any gesture she vanished.

Ferocity fell against the wall in the spare room. Blood ran down her arm and dripped onto the cream carpet. Clutching each hand with the other wasn't easy when they were both mutilated.

She took deep breaths, trying to mellow the pain. She knew she had to get out, leave Earth and get back to Hell. If Fury saw her injuries she might suspect that she'd played a role in all of this.

She fought to get to her feet, but it wasn't working. She felt clammy. She tried to summon the energy to transport herself, but her reserves were empty. She was dizzy.

A black cloud fell over her vision as she slumped to the floor unconscious.

If Baz was dying, he wasn't doing it in a hurry. Norman sat by his side, talking to him as he lay on the ground, still bleeding, the giant spider leg still jammed through his torso. Norman offered to remove the appendage, but Baz said it was the only thing keeping his guts inside his body, so he should "probably leave it."

How is he still alive? Norman wondered.

"It's been a weird couple of days," the one-armed man said.

"It has been a little atypical, I'll give you that."

The last couple days had been a painful reminder of his mortality. Being in a constant state of uncertainty and

147

Model Railway Apocalypse

helplessness had left him feeling like driftwood in a white water river. The idea of joining the sea seemed somehow soothing.

"It's ironic really," Baz said, his eyes struggling to stay open. "I finally make a friend... just in time for the apocalypse."

Norman laughed. Then he registered what Baz had said. He was flattered to be called a friend. Who wouldn't? But the implication that he was the first perturbed him - how closely he could relate. It had been years since he'd had anyone he considered a good friend – unless he counted Fury. It wasn't because he'd tried and failed. He'd just never liked people that much.

"The sentiment is mutual," he finally replied.

"I'm not kidding," Baz went on. "Most people are idiots."

"I agree."

"I mean... here we are at the end of the world... I'm glad I've faced it with someone half-decent."

"Agreed."

It sunk in just how valuable Baz had been to him throughout this ordeal. Norman couldn't imagine now what it would have been like to go through it alone. He didn't want to imagine it. When Fury brought the world to life, she said she'd fashioned it from the essence that Norman had nurtured in his construction. That included the people. So, in a way, Baz was his creation. On placing the miniature figure in the model world he'd unwittingly attached a number of qualities to him – qualities he'd value in a friend: unpretentiousness, earnestness, loyalty and – perhaps ironically – authenticity. These were all the qualities that he valued – qualities that had kept Norman alive.

Luke James

Why hadn't Baz been corrupted along with the rest of the world? Somehow he'd remained untarnished by the changes. Even now, after everything, he was the stalwart companion Norman needed. Was that because of how Norman had created him?

Or was it something to do with Fury?

He was resigned now to the idea that she was gone. And there was a good chance she wouldn't be coming back.

Baz gurgled something and shuffled. Norman realised he'd been in deep thought for too long. He didn't want to seem rude in Baz's final moments, but he couldn't help but wonder about his own future. What would happen to him now? Would he stay lost here in oblivion forever? Was there still some way back? He remembered the idea he'd had about walking to the edge of the world and seeing what happened if he stepped off.

Baz gurgled again.

"Is there anything I can do?" Norman asked.

"Yeah," the large man answered, opening his eyes. "I'm think I'm ready to get up now. Wanna give me a hand?"

Luke James

CHAPTER TWENTY-THREE

It became clear to Norman that Baz was getting up whether it was a good idea or not, even with a giant spider leg impaling his gut. It looked like an awkwardly positioned third leg hanging out of his front. As Norman helped him to his feet he noticed the spiked tip sticking out of his lower back like a tail.

"It's not so bad," Baz said, shuffling on his feet for balance.

"Are you sure?" Norman asked, trying not to show his disbelief.

"Yeah. Lose an arm, gain a leg… and a tail," he said feeling the point at his back. "So what now?" he asked.

Norman was speechless. How was this man still alive? How was he still alive?

"I've no idea," Norman answered.

"I need to meet this wife of yours," Baz said.

Norman nodded, but it was only to be polite. He didn't think there was any chance of it actually happening. Not now.

A train whistle peeped from somewhere far away. Norman and Baz scanned the horizon. The mist was clearing, but it was still too dark to see beyond a hundred meters or so.

"Was that a train?" Baz asked.

"I think so."

The whistle came again, this time louder, accompanied by screeching and shrieking.

Model Railway Apocalypse

"Look up there!" Baz said, pointing at the sky. It was filled with a vast black swarm, coming towards them.

The sky became darker as the swarm came closer. Soon he recognised their red eyes. The demonites. They were flying.

"They don't give up do they?" Baz said. His comment seemed ironic to Norman.

The familiar train whistle rang out again: "Dude-dude!"

Now he could see it. It was coming towards them. But how? There were no rails in this part of town. As he looked closer he saw a large figure sitting atop the locomotive – not as big as the giantess had been, but big. The figure was hunched over the train, riding it like a motorbike.

Demon or not, Norman recognised his wife. She was clad in the armour she'd been wearing the day they met. But now she was ten times the size and straddling the psychotic locomotive. And she looked divine.

"Another giantess?" Baz asked.

"Not exactly," Norman answered, mouth hanging open at the vision. "That's my wife."

"Damn." Baz puffed his cheeks. "We know how to pick 'em, hey?"

Norman nodded.

She's still here, he thought. His heart pounded as his chances of salvation seemed to increase.

"Dude-dude!" the train peeped again.

The swarm swooped and circled around them, flashing their sharp claws and glowing red eyes. For the moment at least, they only seemed intent on intimidation: despite the circling and swooping they hadn't yet struck either man.

But what were Fury's intentions? As she drew closer Norman tried to read her body language. She was hunched

Luke James

forward, poised and determined. From what he could make out, her face conveyed fierce concentration.

Norman swallowed hard.

He saw now how the train was moving where there hadn't been any rails. Two steel strips wiggled and waved in front of it, like tentacles. They were growing longer all the time. As the locomotive approached the steel tentacles spontaneously landed on the ground, forming parallel lines. Fury seemed to be using her god-like powers, telekinetically manipulating the track as if it was an erratic roller-coaster where the track was completed only seconds before the train rattled over it.

The steel strips shimmered in the sky above them, reflecting the fire and chaos.

"Who's that?" Baz asked.

"Where?"

"On the front of the train. There's a normal-sized woman too."

He was right: there was woman chained to the funnel at the front of the train, just above the locomotive's grinning face. It was the barmaid, the real barmaid. She was screaming. Two parallel lines fell to the ground either side of Norman and Baz. Both men gulped. She means to kills us.

"Hey dude!"

Norman pushed Baz to one side and dived to the other, narrowly avoiding the on-coming train. It rattled by at high speed, pulling six carriages in its wake.

When the last carriage passed Norman leapt to his feet and ran towards Baz, who lay safely on the other side of the track.

"You okay?"

Baz sat upright. "Yeah, I think so," he said shaking his

Model Railway Apocalypse

head. "I'm not sure your wife has forgiven you yet."

The train was circling around, tentacle-like tracks forming a wide loop, curving back towards them.

"I'm inclined to agree," Norman replied. "Come on. She's coming back."

Norman helped Baz to his feet and they began shuffling towards the nearest factory. The swarm swooped down, blocking their path. The creatures flashed their claws and hissed through sharp teeth.

The two men ducked down to avoid getting mauled.

Most of the swarm didn't strike at them directly, as though they'd been given orders to hold back. But one particularly aggressive demonite plunged towards them head on. Baz swung his remaining arm, thumping it directly in the face. It was a perfect strike. The creature fell to the ground limp.

"Nice hit," Norman said. It wasn't bad for a man with a giant spider limb sticking through his body like a keyring.

They kept moving.

Norman noticed the swarm clearing, no longer taking fly-bys at such close range. Maybe Baz's punch had deterred them. Or maybe there was some other reason.

A glance to his side and he saw Fury and the locomotive charging again – the screaming barmaid on the front.

Just a bit further to go, Norman told himself.

A deep voice filled the air: "You never mentioned your wife had such firm thighs!" the loco-path quipped. His gleeful face was wedged between them as he gunned forwards with Norman in his sights.

He's right about that, Norman thought. He certainly missed her thighs. Along with the rest of her. Perched atop that train she looked so radiant. So powerful.

Steel rails landed either side of them again.

154

Luke James

"Dude-dude!" the train chirped.

"Jump!" Norman barked. They flung themselves out of the way, scarcely avoiding vehicular annihilation.

Fury and the train passed by with its six clattering carriages in tow.

Norman didn't know which was worse – the overwhelming fear of an excruciating death, or the excruciating notion that his wife was trying to murder him.

The demonites flocked back. This time they seemed more intent on doing harm, nose-diving directly at the two men, who kept moving towards the shelter of the factory. Deep down Norman knew that even if they did reach the building it wouldn't provide much refuge. Fury would just tear it down anyway.

One of the creatures zipped down and slashed their claws along Norman's arm, tearing through his robe and opening up a deep valley in his flesh. Another streaked passed carving at his chest. The pain no longer fazed him. They just added to the divots in his head, the scratches on his face and the huge bite on his shoulder.

"Nearly there!" he shouted to Baz. "Keep going!"

But there was no response. When he glanced to his side, Baz wasn't there.

"Baz?" he called out.

Norman heard a hollering from above. He looked up and saw his friend being carried through the air by four of the winged creatures.

"Don't worry about me, Norman!" he shouted. "You get to safety!"

But Norman knew the truth. There was no safety. Not really. Fury could reshape the world, removing every hiding place and adding more and more terrors.

155

Model Railway Apocalypse

Anyway, did he really want to get to safety? Staying alive didn't seem so appealing when the woman he loved wanted him dead. He couldn't go on running and fighting. He wasn't made for it.

The demonites hovered in the sky, flapping their wings while accosting his only friend. Baz wriggled and writhed, elbowing his way out of their grip and throwing punches every chance he got.

Norman just wanted it to be over.

One vicious demonite tugged the giant appendage from the large man's body. Baz cried out. They dropped him. He spun as he fell to the ground, thumping hard as he landed flat on his back, unconscious.

It was clear Fury wasn't interested in talking to him. There was only one way this could end now.

The track was in the sky, banking around like one end of a velodrome as the train turned to face him once again. For a moment he simply watched, taking in the graceful movement, admiring the way the wind caught his wife's hair which danced and trembled behind her as she rode the steel monster.

The lines of steel quivered and quaked through the air, before settling on the ground in front of him, either side of him, behind him, lining up to turn his bones to powder as the locomotive rushed on. Faster now. Faster than before.

Norman took a deep breath and kept his feel rooted to the ground. His chest pounded as he tried not to think about what he was about to do.

Fury was coming directly at him now. Unblinking, he searched to catch her eye. But she wasn't looking at him, her gaze pointed downwards at the train and the track. Why wasn't she looking? Why wasn't she facing the man she was about to kill?

Luke James

Norman knew why. And he was counting on it.

He stood firm between the rails as she shot towards him. He kept trying to make eye contact.

Come on. Look at me.

He had only seconds for this to work.

The train peeped again. The barmaid screamed. Shrieks filled the sky.

Look at me!

She did. Her fiery eyes glanced up like rising suns, looking directly at him. Norman held her gaze. No matter how firmly his instincts told him to move, he remained. It took all his strength not to leap out of the way. Strength that he'd gained from her. Her eyes. Her monstrous beauty that had kept him going since the moment he'd met her. How quickly it had gone, from that fateful night to this unending one. He'd probably already be dead if she hadn't come along like some guardian angel. He'd certainly been thinking about it. So what difference did it make dying now?

Just twenty two years of joy. Twenty two years. She'd come from Hell and made his twisted Earth feel a little more like Heaven.

He was sorry that it had to end. But thankful all the same. Thankful for the good times.

Bracing himself for the inevitable, he pulled his eyes away from hers and closed them tight.

What is he doing? Why is he just standing there? Twice he'd leapt out of the way. Why not now? Something pulled on her guts. She'd been drunk on her anger and now, no matter how hard she tried to keep hold of it the fire was slipping away. She was sobering up.

He watched her. What are you looking at?

Model Railway Apocalypse

She snarled, trying to fuel the flames but they were fading, wiped out by something entirely more powerful and honest. It made her entire body ache. What was this feeling? Passion or compassion? Abomination or adoration?

Why isn't he moving?

None of this made sense any more. That truth she'd seen in the eyes of the man wrongfully cast into Hell, she could see it now.

He closed his eyes.

Seized by straps of self-doubt, Fury let out a skull-piercing scream.

"Move!" she shouted. But he didn't.

What's this? The large man, the companion stepped between the tracks in front of Norman. Who was this man who'd somehow eluded her influence? Why wasn't he transformed like the others?

No... It can't be...

His eyes glowed yellow. He put his arm out towards her and shook his head.

They're here...

Screaming, Fury strained and twisted the rails, lifting them upwards. The train swerved into the sky.

Seconds after he expected to be dead, an explosion caused Norman to open his eyes. He looked up and saw the contorted rails, pitched skywards and angled directly at the tip of one of the towers. The train itself had been destroyed on impact; its parts scattered and rolled away from its blazing remains.

He could see Fury's giant booted legs sticking out from behind the factory. She moved slowly, her legs folded over one another and shifting like those of a barely conscious

Luke James

teenager passed out at a party.

The swarm had dissipated, flying off into the distance.

Where was Baz? Norman scanned the area.

"Baz!" he called.

But there was no sign of him.

"Baz!" he called again.

Still nothing. His throat ached and his eyes began to burn.

In the corner of his vision, Fury sat upright. He looked at her through gathering tears and crumbled to his knees, no longer able to fight the pain he felt, outside and within.

Fury regarded him through the smoke and tears. How vulnerable he looked. No, not vulnerable. That would suggest he hadn't yet been broken. As he kneeled on the ground, she saw that he'd already been torn to pieces.

That made two of them.

She wanted to say something, but no words came. What words would make this right? She needed time, distance. They both did.

He'd still hurt her, hadn't he? He'd had this coming, hadn't he? This is what happened to sinners.

Even so, the shattered and burned sight of him now – the man she'd loved for over two decades – was enough to make her feel ill.

She got to her feet. After one last glance at her unfortunate husband, she exited the world they'd both created.

Luke James

CHAPTER TWENTY-FOUR

While he was in her custody, Fury was obliged to wait with the human Jeremy until a verdict came back from the judges. He remained strapped to her table in the centre of her pit. In the time she'd been gone, a strange malaise seemed to have crept over him. He was either gazing at the Hellish ceiling of dangling colons, or he was staring into space.

It was awkward. Usually in the time she spent with humans she was either torturing them, healing them ready to torture them again, or mopping them up. She'd never had to just sit with one before.

She wasn't sure how to act, so she perched on the edge of her pit, trying to decide for herself whether or not the unfortunate soul could have been "misdirected". The way he behaved on arrival was unusual. The guilty tended to know they were guilty. There was a realisation that the way they had lived their life had led them to this point. The suffering they'd caused or ignored. The self-interest they'd made a habit of prioritising. Even if they were in denial to start with, the realisation caught up with them eventually, followed swiftly by terror at what was to come. But this one – he'd shown neither denial nor fear. He hadn't resisted or tried to run. He'd been cooperative right from the beginning – maybe even a little courteous. That was an entirely new human quality to Fury. The only real emotion he'd shown was the sadness that now seemed to haunt him. Sadness usually came much later – somewhere

161

Model Railway Apocalypse

in the early stages of redemption.

Now he was muttering something.

What's this? What's he saying? She leaned in closer to listen.

"Somewhere in our rush to get on, we lose track of what we become. Our souls forgotten on the playroom shelves, dancing in the shadows of our once-forever selves."

Fury wasn't sure what it meant. But she liked it.

"What was that?" she asked.

For the first time his eyes focused on something. Focused on her as she approached the table.

"It's a poem," he said.

"A poem?"

"Yeah."

"What's a poem?"

"It's a moment wrapped in words," he said, smiling.

"What does it mean?" she asked.

"Whatever you want it to." He paused, his smile fading again. "To me it's about regret... I suppose."

"What do you regret?"

Fury hoped it might give her a clue as to why he was in Hell.

"Accepting death so easily," he said.

Luke James

CHAPTER TWENTY-FIVE

He wished he hadn't been so cowardly in those final moments when he'd closed his eyes. He'd heard a scream, the twisting and grinding of metal, and the harrowing explosion. He'd watched Fury disappear and there was still no sign of Baz. No body. Nothing from the man who - in this seemingly endless night - had played the part of his guardian angel.

Alone now, he perched on the fallen body of the giant robot, his face smeared with coal and his flannel robe stained with a cocktail of shark and dinosaur guts. He surveyed the toy box of nightmares around him. An unnatural green glow spilled out of the river and mangled corpses were sprawled across the banks, mutated and contorted. The hills, once the colour of spring, were coated with ash, and lava still oozed sluggishly from the highest peak.

How long had it been here now? It was hard to count the days when there seemed to be nothing but night. When had he last seen daylight? He couldn't see anyone left alive, but disembodied groans told him they were out there, in the shadows beyond the whispering train wreck – lost souls with no say over their fate, caught in an epic domestic through no fault of their own. In a way they were his children, and he was their God, stripped of his power and banished to live among them, in his own creation.

How long had it been? Too long. There was nothing left to do.

Model Railway Apocalypse

He slid off the deceased mechanoid and began his slow, final walk to the edge of the world.

The spare room was a little more crowded than Fury had expected. Greeted by the warm embrace of her daughter, she felt as if she was crawling out of a deep, dreaming sleep. Having lost track of time she was surprised to see Malice.

"Mother!" Malice said, hugging her tightly. Her body was rigid and her voice uncertain. Over her shoulder, Fury saw her soon-to-be son-in-law, Henry, watching her apprehensively.

What's wrong with them? she wondered.

Fury realised Henry had never seen her in full demon form. Surely he'd seen Malice with a similar appearance?

He waved awkwardly, holding a rolled up bandage in his hand. He glanced at the floor with a frown.

"What's going on?" Fury asked.

"We were going to ask the same thing," Malice said, pulling away from their embrace and gesturing to the corner of the room.

Fury realised what was happening. Her mother was collapsed and unconscious against the wall, hands caked in blood. She was naked.

"What the...?" Fury muttered. She followed the trail of blood from Ferocity back to the model world.

"We arrived five minutes ago. Let ourselves in when there was no answer. We found her here."

Fury crouched next to her mother. She nudged her shoulders and Ferocity stirred. When her eyes finally focused on Fury, she jolted uncomfortably.

Fury wondered what was going on. Something wasn't right. What was her mother doing here? Why was she

Luke James

covered in blood? Why did the trail lead back to the town?

Ferocity shuffled awkwardly while Fury regarded her with suspicious eyes.

Henry knelt down, offering to bandage Ferocity's hand; she batted him aside. Fury noticed the missing digits.

"Grandma!" Malice snapped, reproachfully. "He's only trying to help!"

"I don't need help from a human," Ferocity said, scowling.

"Why are you here?" Fury demanded.

She didn't answer.

"Were you in there?" Fury pointed at the model world.

Still no answer. But Ferocity's malicious grimace told her she'd been involved somehow.

Fury grabbed her by the neck and lifted her off the ground, pinning her against the wall.

"Speak, you bitch!"

"What are you doing?" Malice gasped.

"Getting the truth!" Fury bellowed, thumping her mother against the wall. "What have you done?"

Drowsily, Ferocity simply smiled. "What I needed to do."

Fury threw her across the room. She hit the wall and started laughing. Fury turned back to the model world.

What had she done?

Everything she'd put Norman through. There was more to this and she needed to get to the bottom of things.

"You think he's going to take you back now?" Ferocity chided.

Fury swung a punch at her mother. Her fist went through the wall as Ferocity ducked out of the way. Fury watched as she ran across the room and dived once more into the miniature world.

Norman! Fury had to protect him. Whatever Fercocity did, it wouldn't end well for him.

165

Model Railway Apocalypse

Malice grabbed Fury by the shoulders. "What's going on?"

"It's your father! He's trapped in there and we need to save him!"

Fury squinted at the model. Where was he? She couldn't see his light. Either it was too faint for her panicked eyes, or he was already dead.

Where is he?

"Help me!" Fury shouted, grabbing her daughter's hand. Together they leapt into Furydale.

Luke James

CHAPTER TWENTY-SIX

Norman sat with his feet dangling over the edge of the world. He'd picked a point on the horizon and walked through the mists, across the ash-covered ground. Early on in his ordeal he'd wondered what would happen if he walked and kept on walking. He knew that – unlike the Earth – this world was flat and finite. He'd sanded the edges himself.

As he'd left the town and stepped over the train tracks, crossed the river-bridge and walked between the trees, the horizon hadn't appeared to come any closer, much like an old video game. It wasn't so much a horizon, as a 360 degree painting, an ambient impression of a world beyond Furydale. It was beautiful – with a crimson sun now sitting flush with the land - but it had faded and disintegrated as Norman walked further and further away from the town, replaced with neither darkness nor light, just white noise like a dead television channel.

So what would happen if he jumped? Would he die? Disappear from existence? Or be returned back to the real world? Norman was getting ready to find out.

He stood up and stared over the edge. He'd been looking into an abyss when he'd met Fury –not a physical one, but a metaphorical one. He'd lost both his parents and the world had been closing around him. Then she'd come along and changed everything. He had a meaning and a purpose. Something to hold onto. He'd always known it could slip away easily. The last twenty two years had felt

167

Model Railway Apocalypse

like borrowed time.

At least he was leaving a piece of himself behind. He wished he could see Malice again, happy and excited for her future. She deserved it all. What would she think? Would she ever know the truth? Would Fury work out what really happened eventually?

Norman sighed and shuffled his feet, peering into the abyss. There had to be another way. His mouth felt dry.

He heard a bark. He turned to see a sheepdog running towards him. It was the sheepdog from the park who'd been playing with children the first time he'd entered Furydale.

How the hell have you survived all this time? he wondered. The dog stopped at his feet, wagging its tail.

Norman patted him.

"Good boy," he said. The dog lapped up the attention.

Can I really do this with the dog watching? Norman asked himself. He looked over the edge again.

"Do it," came a gravelly voice from behind him.

The dog whimpered and ran away.

So much for man's best friend.

Norman knew who it was, even before he turned around to see her still clutching her mutilated hands. Her hair was black – blacker than he remembered. Far blacker than Fury's.

"Maybe you can join me," he said coolly, unfazed that she was completely naked. This woman had taken everything from him and put him through a nightmare, but he wasn't going to let her see him angry.

"I'll pass," she said with a smirk. "Not even I know what you'll find down there."

"It's got to be better than what's up here," he said. "How are your hands?"

168

Luke James

Ferocity raised her middle finger at him. "This one still works," she said. "You gonna jump or what?"

"They don't teach reverse psychology in Hell, do they?"

"What do you mean?"

"I mean if you want someone to do something, you don't tell them to do it. You tell them do to the opposite."

"Okay. Right" Ferocity rolled her eyes. "Oh please, don't do it. Don't jump."

"Ah-hah! See? Now you've got it."

"So what? Is it working?"

"No. But thanks for humouring me."

"Screw this," Ferocity said, getting impatient. She raised her tail over her shoulder and pointed it at him.

"I meant to ask..." Norman began, stalling for time. "Why do you hate me so much?"

Ferocity snorted.

"Don't take it personally," she said. "I hate all humans."

"I'm not a big fan of them either," Norman said. "Why do you think I fell in love with your daughter?"

"Ick! Spare me." She rolled her eyes.

"You might stink as a person... but you did a good job raising her."

"Thank you, I suppose," Ferocity said. "It was going well until you came along."

"Sorry about that."

"You should be," she said. Without any more hesitation, she shot a burst of magic and sent him over the edge.

Luke James

CHAPTER TWENTY-SEVEN

It was all too easy. Ferocity knew getting rid of the husband would damage her relationship with her daughter and her granddaughter, but forever was a long time and time was the greatest healer - both would forgive her eventually. It would only be a temporary inconvenience.

Talking of which, as she leant over the edge of the world, she saw Norman still clinging on by his fingers.

She peered over the rim and met his eye. His face was red as he worked to maintain his grip.

"You really are like a bogey on a finger," she sneered.

"Better a bogey on the finger," he said straining, "than a fissure in the scrotum."

"Ah-hah! One of my favourite forms of torture!" she said. "Amazingly effective on males."

Norman pulled himself up, lifting his elbow over the edge for balance. With a shove of her blue foot she knocked his arm away, leaving him barely clinging on once again. His groan was pathetic.

She placed her foot onto his fingers and shifted her weight, crushing them.

Norman heard his bones cracking. He felt the strength running out of them, replaced with numbness.

She licked her lips and raised her tail again, this time slashing it at his fingers, drawing blood from his knuckles. The warmth ran down his hands and down his wrists.

It's over, he told himself.

Model Railway Apocalypse

He closed his eyes, mentally preparing to let go.

A foul scream filled the air. The pressure disappeared from his fingers. Norman opened his eyes and Ferocity was gone.

Where is she?

He dangled from the edge of the world. He no longer had the energy to lift himself up. But something was going on. His arms felt like iron, refusing to respond. Come on, he told himself. Move.

But it wouldn't work. He was spent.

Then he saw Fury's face, looking down at him.

I'm seeing things. I'm already dead. He blinked several times, trying to confirm what he saw.

No. I'm not dead yet. But it's not her. It's still her mother. He convinced himself Ferocity was imitating Fury just to torture him some more. Another cruel joke. A final jibe, reminding him how she'd tricked him not once, but twice. Never again.

Fury reached down. She grabbed his arms and lifted him from the edge. When she placed him back down on terra firma he struggled out of her grip, and retreated, eying her suspiciously. It was as though he didn't recognise her. As though she were a stranger.

I suppose I deserve that, she told herself. After everything she knew she shouldn't be surprised that he no longer trusted her.

"Norman," she began, not knowing what she was going to say.

"Get away from me!" he shouted. "I know it's not you!"

Not me? What did he mean? The way he looked at her – it was as though he was searching her face for something... His eyes were bold and manic.

Luke James

"Norman, it's me! Who else would I be?" she reached out towards him.

He simply jerked backwards like an abused puppy.

Then he looked at her hands. He grabbed her by the wrists and pulled her hands up to his face. He gazed at them in disbelief.

"What is it?" Fury asked.

"Your hands," he muttered - his voice shaky. "Your fingers...."

What did he mean? Fury's stomach knotted. Her muscles tensed and her heart thumped. No. It couldn't be true. She felt lightheaded as she realised he was surprised she still had her fingers. She replayed his earlier comment in her mind: it's not you. Who did he think she was?

But she knew the answer.

She turned back to her mother, who lay on the ground, propping herself up on her elbows. She was watching as Fury put the pieces together.

"Dad!" Malice called out. "You found him!" She ran to Norman's side and hugged him tightly. Norman accepted her embrace, albeit hesitantly.

Fury turned back to Ferocity.

"You!" she snarled. "You set this whole thing up!"

Ferocity answered with only a smile.

Fury ran at her, lifting her off her feet. She raised her tail and pointed it at her mother.

Ferocity laughed.

"What are you going to do, my wayward daughter? Use your magic on me? I still know your secret. You can't touch me with your powers. I'll keep coming back again and again until this nauseating marriage is over."

Fury knew her mother was right. She couldn't get rid of Ferocity while she still kept her secret from Norman. She

173

Model Railway Apocalypse

looked at her husband, who lay collapsed on the ground, propped up by their daughter, who was tending to his wounds, healing him with magic.

Could she tell him? Would it spell the end of their family?

"Go on," Ferocity said, as if reading her mind. "Tell all. Even if he does take you back after all of this, he'll never keep you once he knows the truth about you. Once he knows the whole story about how your repulsive relationship came into being."

At that, Malice lay her father down on the ground and approached Fury.

"What's going on?" the young demoness asked. "What truth?"

"I have to tell your father something," Fury said. Heaviness pulled at her shoulders and tightness seized her chest. "Or we'll never be free of her."

"Tell him what? He can barely keep himself upright. Tell him what?"

"Do it!" Ferocity snapped.

Fury knew she had no choice. So long as Ferocity had leverage over her, there was nothing to stop her trying something like this again. Fury needed to be able to cast her mother out once and for all.

"Watch her," Fury said to Malice. "Don't let her go anywhere."

Fury walked over to Norman. He lay on his back, gazing up at the deepening black sky. His eyes turned to her as she stepped into view. The panic was gone. He seemed defeated - resigned to whatever fate had left for him.

She crouched down at his side.

"Norman," she began.

He blinked.

"I know you probably hate me now. But I need to tell you

Luke James

something. It's going to be painful for you to hear. But for both our sakes you need to hear it."

He stared at her with dull eyes. His hands rested on his chest. She picked them up and held them in her own.

He didn't flinch. That's a good sign.

"Remember the man I told you about? The one who came to me by mistake?"

Norman blinked again.

"It was your father."

Somewhere in the background, Malice gasped. Ferocity snorted. But Norman still looked at her blankly.

"He was the innocent man damned. I swear to Lucifer I had him removed as soon as I realised the mistake. But you have to know this. He was the first good man I'd ever encountered. The gentlest soul I'd ever met. I'd never known human kindness until the night he fell into my pit.

"In the short time we had together, waiting for the verdict on his future, he broke through my defences, telling me about his life on Earth. About you. God, how he loved you Norman. How he worried about you being on your own after he'd gone. I could only listen as he told me about his wonderful, creative son. His son who always thought of others and had so much love to give - who'd helped him through losing his wife. I had to meet you for myself.

"I risked everything doing what I did. But your father had shown me a light. A single floating candle in an ocean of darkness. I had to get a closer look at the glow. And I haven't gone back since."

Fury's self-loathing was in overdrive. How despicable I am trying to make what happened sound poetic. She winced when she considered what he must think of her now.

Tears gathered in his eyes. In them, she saw her own

175

Model Railway Apocalypse

reflection. Little windows showing both his pain and the cause.

"After everything I've put you through, I know you must hate me. I never told you any of that before because I knew it would kill you to think of your father in Hell. I haven't told you now to simply make myself feel better. I did it to protect you. I understand if you want me out of your life."

She felt Ferocity and Malice's dual gazes on her back. But she kept her eyes locked on Norman, waiting for some kind of response.

"Let me take you away from here," she said. "Then I'll leave you alone. Okay?"

Still no response.

"Please say something."

Norman cleared his throat and swallowed.

"Hate you?" he said, shaking his head. "How could I hate you?"

Her vision became blurry. She hadn't noticed the gathering tears in her own eyes. They ran onto his face as she leant over and kissed him.

Her hair was smoky as it fell over his face. He closed his eyes and breathed it in deeply while she kissed him, as though he was breathing in life itself. God, how he'd missed it. How he'd missed her.

He felt her hand on his cheek as she pulled away. This time when he opened his eyes, hers remained closed. She rubbed her lips together as if savouring the kiss.

"I'm so sorry," she said, putting her hand on his shoulder. He flinched, pulling her hand away.

"What is it?" she asked.

Norman pulled the robe off his shoulder, revealing the jagged wound. "Raptor bite," he said. He'd never

Luke James

considered himself particularly macho, but couldn't help but grin.

"What!" came an angry voice from behind them. "You're forgiving her?"

Ferocity got to her feet and stormed towards them, raising her trail. Fury jumped up, and did the same.

"It's a standoff then," Ferocity said.

"Not quite," Malice said, pointing her tail at her grandmother. "It's two verses one."

Norman felt a pang of pride and a surge of relief as he watched his family stand up to Ferocity.

"Malice, darling! What are you thinking?" Ferocity pleaded.

"I'm thinking I want to take my dad home. And I want you to leave."

"So do I!" Fury added.

Together, mother and daughter shot a blast of magic. Ferocity lit up like a lightbulb. She thrashed and screamed as the fiery glow consumed her, before finally, she disappeared from the model world, from the Earth, back to Hell.

Now, with his wife and daughter back at his side, Norman felt invincible.

"Let's get you home," Fury said.

Luke James

CHAPTER TWENTY-EIGHT

The decision had been made: the human Jeremy was to be "reallocated". Very little would be said about the maladministration. The sorting process was firmly regarded as "perfect". Even though those she'd spoken to had confirmed "mistakes do happen", the consensus was that it wasn't to be "bandied about".

The powers that be were coming to get him. They would be here soon. Fury untied him.

"Thank you," he said, sitting up slowly and rubbing his wrists.

She perched back on the edge of the pit and crossed her arms.

"What you said before," Fury began, "about accepting death so easily. What did you mean?"

Fury was fascinated by the idea of death – or rather, a finite life.

To her surprise, the human got up off the table and sat down next to her, as if they were drinking companions.

"Well..." he said. "Life becomes heavier the older you get. Friends and family start to pass away, your bones aren't so strong. You become ill. Simply standing up becomes exhausting. There are times when carrying on feels like harder and harder work. And a part of you longs for the next stage. Whatever it might be." He glanced at his surroundings again.

Fury had never considered what it felt like to age as humans did.

Model Railway Apocalypse

"Poetry is one of the ways some people cope with the idea of death. Others use music or art... or religion. Do you have those here?"

Fury shook her head.

"That's a shame."

For demons, justice was a way of life, while angels embraced love as the highest order. But this human seemed to imply that the inevitable promise of death served to nurture a wisdom and insight among their kind.

"I lost my wife two years ago. She got ill and died within weeks. I knew back then that I'd soon follow. But my son helped me to keep on going. He held things together when it was all falling apart. He gave me reason to keep going. Gave me two more years of joy."

He took a long breath.

"I kept on going for him. But I couldn't go on forever. In the end I embraced death as though I was boarding a train."

"And you regret that?" Fury asked.

"I suppose regret is the wrong word. But it was hard letting go knowing that I'd be leaving him on his own. I'm worried about him. He doesn't have many people close to him, or anyone as far as I know. He tends to keep himself to himself. A bit of a dreamer, you might say. More interested in reading than socialising."

"You said you didn't spend enough time with him..."

"There's never enough time in the world to spend with people you care about."

Fury looked up and saw The Powers that Be walking across the overpass – cloaked demons who wore masks of shadow and rarely spoke.

She became suddenly aware of what she was doing: she was having a conversation with a human - a human who

Luke James

wasn't afraid of her – who was talking to her as though she were a friend. Most alarming was that she was enjoying listening to him. He'd only existed for a blink of a demon eye, but his eyes were full of experience. His voice croaked as he spoke about life and death. Fury got the impression he'd spent a lot of time reflecting. Demons weren't encouraged to reflect.

The Powers that Be were approaching the edge of her pit.

Fury still had more questions. She was surprised to find herself wishing she had longer with him. She supposed she could ask the next damned soul, but there was something about this one. Was it the way he reflected on things that kept him free of damnation? She had to know more. But it was too late.

There were three of them. They were entering the pit now.

"What happens now?" the human asked.

Fury watched as two demons apprehended him and the other pulled a rock out of his pouch. He ran his hand over the stone and it began to glow. Then he let go and it remained floating in mid-air. Fury had never seen this before.

The demon with the stone placed his fingertips together on either side, then pulled his hands apart. The glow spread out, becoming a shining portal the size of a human.

"You walk through," Fury finally answered, as the demons positioned him.

"Where am I going?" he asked.

Fury felt a tugging in her chest. The demons pushed him towards the portal.

"Wherever you want," she said.

He stepped forward as instructed, turning around at the

Model Railway Apocalypse

final step.

"Thank you for your hospitality," he said.

Watching him go, she tried not to smile almost as hard as she tried not to cry.

Luke James

EPILOGUE

Norman was in the spare room, making the final repairs to the model railway. It had been three weeks since what they now affectionately referred as "the little misunderstanding." Ferocity hadn't returned. Fury had assured Norman that her magic would prevent the demon mother-in-law from ever returning to their home uninvited.

"Woo!" she cheered as she entered the room carrying a perfectly baked Victoria sponge and a pot of tea. "I didn't burn it this time!"

"Well done, angel," he said. "That's brilliant."

In Norman's mind, there had never been any question about whether or not he would take Fury back. He'd spent his whole ordeal wanting to get back home. Fury was his home. Returning to the real world would have been pointless if she wasn't there with him.

"Would you like a slice?"

"Yes please."

Of course, he'd never deliberately give her reason to be upset with him, but there was no denying he became extra vigilant in making sure nothing threatened their happiness again. Simple "pleases" and "thank yous" were a small part of that.

He'd never got around to giving her the flowers he'd carried through Hell for her. There had been very little left of them anyway. But that wouldn't be a problem; he'd added another florist to Furydale 2.0.

Model Railway Apocalypse

Between him and Fury they had managed to restore the model railway to virtually the same state it had been before the "misunderstanding", although Norman had re-laid the surface with, bought new model buildings and replaced the trains with new locomotives. Fury had used a dapple of magic to return the people to their previous state.

Norman removed the thick lenses from his eyes and they sat together, drinking tea and eating cake.

"Malice called earlier," Fury said, sipping from her flowery-patterned china tea cup. "They're going to have an Autumn wedding."

"Lovely!" Norman said. "I suppose that means we can go away for the whole summer?"

"Yes it does!" Fury replied. "Any ideas where you fancy going?"

"I've had one or two ideas," Norman said, winking.

They scoffed down the rest of their cake and glugged down their tea.

"Are you ready?" Fury asked, sliding her suitcase out from under the workbench.

"You bet," Norman replied, taking off his dirty shirt, revealing a number of scars across his chest and shoulders. He placed the shirt on a hook on the back of the door where another hung. He picked up the fresher shirt and put it on.

Fury stepped forward and buttoned it up for him.

"You sure you want to do this?" she asked.

"Why on Earth wouldn't I?"

She did up the last of his buttons and kissed him.

"Let's go then." She raised her tail and wrapped it around his wrist.

With a nod of her head, the loving couple zapped back into Furydale.

Luke James

The scene in the park was even more beautiful than before. The sun shone brighter. The grass glowed greener. And the addition of a dinosaur zoo would make for an excellent day out. The giant robot street cleaner would ensure the town remained immaculate while the giantess made sure everyone stayed safe.

Norman and Fury made their way to The – recently renovated – Shaggy Dog.

The appropriately dressed barman served them a glass of red wine and a Stormy Sea. He also handed them their room key.

Before heading upstairs, they decided to sit down by the fireplace to enjoy their drinks.

Norman searched the room with excited eyes, looking out for Baz. Shortly after they'd returned to the real world three weeks ago, Fury had assured him that she could bring back all the citizens of Furydale. Norman was excited to see his baby-faced friend again. He figured this was where he'd find the large man.

But Norman couldn't see him.

"Any sign of your friend?" Fury asked.

"Not yet," Norman said. He knew he must be here. Only that morning he'd positioned the merry patron with the pint glass inside The Shaggy Dog.

Where is he?

The door to the gents opened, and out he stepped, with all four limbs and smiling like a baby covered in goo. He was even carrying his pint glass. Had he actually taken it to the toilet with him?

"Baz!" Norman jumped up and ran over, wrapping his arms around the large man. "It's so good to see you!"

"Hey buddy," Baz replied, slightly alarmed. "Do I know you?"

185

Model Railway Apocalypse

Norman was seized by a sinking feeling.

"Of course you do," he said. "You probably don't recognise me in proper clothes."

Baz smiled, oblivious.

"Ah…. Right…. Yeah," he said, clearly trying to be polite.

Why doesn't he know me? Norman thought.

Fury placed her arm around him and led him back to the armchairs by the fire place.

"Why doesn't he recognise me? I thought you said they'd be restored."

"I did," Fury said. "But I've had a theory about him for a while. I wasn't sure about it until now."

"What theory? What are you talking about?" Norman felt his eyes welling up.

"Your friend, Baz. I think I understand now why he didn't turn like everyone else in the town – why he stuck by you the whole time."

"Why?"

"He was an angel. Or rather, he was inhabited by an angel. They can detect when demons use magic recklessly on Earth. I think he came to protect you. He was the reason I could see where you were from outside the model railway. When he left, I couldn't see you anymore."

Norman felt a shiver. Could it be true?

"I think he was keeping you safe until we worked things out – until I came to my senses."

Norman was speechless.

"I'm so glad that he did," she said. "Or I might have lost you forever."

"Me too," he answered.

Norman knew he had work to do. Their problems hadn't simply gone away with Ferocity. Fury was a little lost, and he'd spent too long drifting and not holding her hand. Yes,

Luke James

she'd come from hell and saved his life, but that was the old story of them. It was followed by the story of raising Malice. But this more recent story of them had taught him not to take anything for granted. They both had needs. The next story would be whatever they crafted together. He needed to pay her the same attention to detail as he had paid when creating the miniature world. And he'd start by asking her what she needed.

He glanced at the new Baz, who'd resumed his drinking by the bar. The merry patron looked over at Norman and raised his glass with a wink.

Luke James

ACKNOWLEDGEMENTS

Thank you to my wife, Sophie, for the continuous love and support. To my parents, Paula and Bern, who could not have been more loving and supportive. To my children, Arthur and Rose, for rocking my world (in every sense). To my father-in-law Steve, for the encouragement to self-publish and my mother-in-law Michelle, for not taking it personally.

Luke James

ABOUT THE AUTHOR

Luke James is an English and Media teacher in the South of England who hopes his students don't read this. This is his first novel.

He can be found on X @Luke_out_world

Printed in Great Britain
by Amazon